## "JANE JEFFRY IS A CROSS BETWEEN MISS MARPLE AND ERMA BOMBECK"

*Mysteries By Mail*

## GRIME AND PUNISHMENT

**"A WINNER"**
Elizabeth Peters

**"IRRESISTIBLE"**
*Alfred Hitchcock's Mystery Magazine*

## A FAREWELL TO YARNS

"Downright clever . . . A quick, fun read."
*Kansas City Star*

"A delightful mystery romp"
Carolyn G. Hart

## A QUICHE BEFORE DYING

"A funny and gripping story
of Midwestern suburban manners,
mores and murder . . .
Jill Churchill is as good at clever plots
as she is at witty titles . . .
GREAT FUN."
Digby Diehl, *Prodigy*

Jane #4

# The Class Menagerie

## JILL CHURCHILL

AVON BOOKS NEW YORK

THE CLASS MENAGERIE is an original publication of Avon Books. This work has never before appeared in book form. This work is a novel. Any similarity to actual persons or events is purely coincidental.

AVON BOOKS
A division of
The Hearst Corporation
1350 Avenue of the Americas
New York, New York 10019

**3 6626 10117 568 5**

Copyright © 1994 by The Janice Young Brooks Trust
Published by arrangement with the author
Library of Congress Catalog Card Number: 93-91667
ISBN: 0-380-77380-5

First Avon Books Printing: February 1994

AVON TRADEMARK REG. U.S. PAT. OFF. AND IN OTHER COUNTRIES, MARCA REGISTRADA, HECHO EN CANADA

Printed in Canada

UNV   10   9   8   7   6   5   4   3

# PROLOGUE

The woman glanced once again at the invitation, then folded the sheet and tapped it thoughtfully against the palm of her hand while she stared out the window.

A class reunion. Good God!

At first, her impulse had been to wad it up and throw it away without even reading beyond the heading:

### "COME TO THE AID OF YOUR OLD SCHOOL!!!"

And even now, she thought that throwing it away was probably the best thing to do.

Still—

In one way, it would be interesting, on a purely intellectual level, to see how they'd all turned out. Had the bright ones used their brains? Had the ambitious ones made anything of themselves? Had the beautiful ones kept their looks? What about the dumb girls, the painfully shy ones? Not much question there. Losers went on losing.

But mild curiosity wasn't reason enough to risk going. What if her presence aroused their old curiosities? Made them ask questions, put suspicions together? They were all, without knowing it, so dangerous to her.

She couldn't help that happening. But if she were there—if she saw conversations and thoughts going in the wrong direction—she could head them off. Change the subject. Create a diversion. Whatever was necessary.

She opened the sheet back up and read carefully. The club members were to go in early and stay with Shelley Nowack.

Who the hell was Shelley Nowack? Oh, yes. That drippy, shy girl.

"I'll do anything, Jane. Anything you ask. I'll give you your next ten perms without bitching a bit. I'll give your name and take your Pap tests. I'll drive your car pools for a year. Name your price," Shelley Nowack said.

Jane Jeffry stared across the kitchen table at her neighbor. "Shelley, you have to tell me what the favor is before I can name a price. This sounds enormous. You want me to adopt your children? Or are you trying to beat me into being president of the PTA? If that's it, there's not a favor in the world you could offer."

"Worse!" Shelley said miserably.

"Nothing's worse!" Jane exclaimed. "Except maybe driving for a junior high field trip. And if that's it, the answer's absolutely no—not for anything."

"It's nothing to do with kids." Shelley ran her fingers through her short cap of neat black hair. This was serious. Jane had never seen Shelley allow a hair out of place. Moreover, Jane's big orange cat Meow had jumped into Shelley's lap and Shelley, who loathed cats, was absentmindedly stroking its fur.

"Let me explain from the beginning. It's not really my fault. Well, it is, of course. But I mean—"

"Shelley, you normally have the disciplined *sang

*froid* of an old-fashioned Mother Superior. It's scary seeing you this way. Get on with it!"

"Yes. Yes, of course!" Shelley said, apparently giving herself a mental slap. "All right. It's like this. You know about this class reunion of mine that's coming up next weekend?" She was still petting Meow.

"Yeah, the weird one that's being held in September instead of spring like everybody else's."

"I explained that to you. The school had a terrible fire and the reunion's being held early so we can get some alumni fund-raising efforts started."

"Uh-huh. Go on."

"Well, there was a girl's club in my school. We did charitable things. Volunteered to decorate for school dances, collected for the United Way, managed phone committees on snow days, that sort of thing. It was quite an honor to be invited to join."

"Why does this sound so harmless and sweet?" Jane asked.

"I was lulled into complacency, too. See, I started thinking about this old club and decided it would be a good idea for the members of the club to meet early and take on the leadership of the fund-raising project to rebuild the school. Appropriate, really."

"Makes sense to me—so far," Jane said warily.

"Here comes the hideous part. I sent out invitations to everybody. I had an old roster of the club that I'd kept updated . . ."

"Of course you had," Jane said. She couldn't even find her current address book half the time, let alone keep old rosters updated, but she and Shelley were cut from a different cloth. Jane's was usually unraveling at the edges.

"I told them we should meet early," Shelley went on. "The reunion actually starts on Friday. It's a three-day deal. And I said we should meet on Wednesday and Thursday before everyone else gets here—"

"We're talking about Wednesday and Thursday of next week, right?"

"Yes. Well, Jane, I thought there'd only be two or three of them available. On our tenth reunion there were only a couple from the club. So—" she drew a deep breath and plunged forward, "so I invited them to stay at my house."

Jane looked at her, perplexed. "And?"

"And I called the class president, Trey Moffat, this morning to see how many beds I need to make up and the son of a bitch casually mentioned that seven of my club members have agreed to come. Seven, Jane! That's an absolute swarm of women! I only sent them all a note as a courtesy and asked them to make suggestions by mail in advance if they wanted. Doesn't anybody these days know an insincere invitation when they see one? What's the world coming to?"

"Seven? Where will you put them all? Oh—you need extra space and you want me to bed some of them down in rows in my basement. By the way, you have a cat on your lap."

"I what? Oh, ick!" Shelley said, dislodging Meow as though he carried a fatal virus. "No, I don't want you to keep them. That crossed my mind, but between us we don't have room for seven and it isn't fair to invite people to your house then make them rough it that way. I've made other arrangements." She was frantically brushing orange fur off her black slacks.

"Good. So where does the favor come in?"

"Well, it's this way—you know Edgar North and Gordon Kane?"

"The men who bought the old Judge Francisco mansion? I've met them. Edgar gave me a recipe for—"

"Those are the ones. They're turning the mansion into a bed and breakfast. They've finally nagged the zoning board into agreeing and the place is almost ready to open for business. So I'm going to open it with my crowd. I'm paying for all of them, so nobody ought to be able to object."

Jane poured herself some more coffee and silently waved the pot in front of Shelley, who nodded. "Shelley, I must be getting awfully dim, but I still don't see a favor looming on the horizon. Sounds to me like you've got everything under control—as usual."

"This is it, Jane—Edgar and Gordon haven't got a staff. They hadn't really planned on opening for a couple weeks—"

Jane's eyes opened very wide. "Oh! I get it! You want me to skivvy!"

"Only breakfast preparation and clean up. And maybe help change bedding. Do a tad of vacuuming. See, Edgar doesn't want to hire anyone in a desperate hurry just to satisfy my need. He wants to take the time to get just the right person. Naturally, Edgar will do most of the work in the kitchen. He just needs you around to help out a little bit."

"Well, housework isn't my favorite thing, but I do make a mean scrambled egg. Sure, I'll help. It would only be a couple of hours for a couple of days. I'd say two perms ought to about even it out. Shelley, what a build up. This isn't nearly as bad as you made me think."

"That isn't the *real* favor," Shelley said.

Jane sat her coffee cup down. "Oh?"

"No, the real favor is, I want you to hang around the rest of the time. To attend with me."

"Go to *your* class reunion! You've lost your mind. I didn't even go to my own!"

"Yes, but I remember why. You said you'd only been at the school you graduated from for six months and you never knew the people and—"

"I hate the way you remember everything I tell you. I probably didn't add this remark at the time: even if I'd known them intimately, I wouldn't have gone. I hate the concept of class reunions. Everybody dieting like mad, getting face-lifts and having family pictures taken to show off. I've known people who spent the better part of a year before a reunion getting a fake life together to show off."

"But you don't have to fake anything for this. You didn't know them."

"Why in the world would you want me to go to your reunion?"

"Well, Jane, it's this way—I was terribly shy in high school—"

Jane laughed. "Try another one. You're about as shy as Attila the Hun."

Shelley's eyebrows went up. "You didn't know me then. I was hideously shy. Almost phobic."

"Shelley, this is like being told that the Pope used to be an arms dealer. It won't fly. You can't possibly expect me to believe this of a woman who has the entire school board, city council, and neighborhood jumping through hoops."

Shelley preened a little. "Not exactly through hoops."

"So, even if you were shy, what has it got to do with the reunion? You're not a fading violet anymore."

"I think that's 'shrinking' violet. If you're going to speak in clichés, you ought to get them right."

"Don't be snappish with me. I've got the upper hand for a change," Jane said with a grin.

Shelley took a delicate sip of her coffee while she mentally marshaled her forces. "Jane, if you've never been to a reunion, this will seem strange to you. But when I went to my tenth, I went striding in with complete confidence and was suddenly overcome by the person I used to be. It's as if someone pressed a button and I dropped through the floor into a time warp—ten years fell away as if they'd never happened and I was that same stammering twerp I used to be."

"You're kidding!"

"And I'm afraid it'll happen again. I need you there, Jane, to constantly remind me what a bossy bitch I really am."

"You mean, what a confident, liberated woman you are."

Shelley nodded. "Whatever. Anyway, if you're there helping Edgar and Gordon, it's a perfect excuse to sort of hang around. And you can be my 'date' for the other school stuff, the picnic and the dance."

"Why isn't Paul your date? Husbands are said to be good for that sort of thing."

"Paul's out of town. Out of the country, as a matter of fact, and I think it's because of this thing. He went to the tenth with me and hated it so much that he gave me that sapphire tennis bracelet on the condition that I never mention the word reunion to him again."

"It was that bad?"

"*No!* No, not really, but he was coming down with the flu and felt miserable and it colored his whole memory. It wasn't really bad, he's just remembering it through a haze of decongestants."

"I'll bet."

"I'll loan you the bracelet anytime you want if you'll do this for me."

Jane waved this away. "I wouldn't trust myself to wear something that expensive. Why are they called tennis bracelets anyway? You'd have to be crazy to wear something like that on a tennis court. If you got hot and sweaty, it could fly right off—"

"Jane!"

"Sorry. Let me see what's on next week." She rose and went to the calendar over the kitchen phone. "I've got grade school car pool mornings, Back-to-School night on Thursday. I could probably trade for afternoon car pools, but it would be a two-for-one deal. Nobody wants mornings. But for my very best friend who is going to trade me for a fabulous favor, to be named later—"

"How fabulous?" Shelley asked.

"Fabulous in direct ratio to the horribleness of the reunion."

"It won't be horrible," Shelley said. "In fact, it might be kind of fun."

"Wanna bet? So, what's this club called?"

Shelley squirmed. "You don't want to know."

"More horrible confessions? Come on. Devastate me!"

Shelley mumbled into her coffee cup. "The Ewe Lambs."

*"Ewe Lambs?"* Jane shrieked with delight.

"It wasn't our fault! The football team was the Rams and the club was formed ten years before I was even in high school."

"And I'll bet you had cute stuff like, 'Do ewe solemnly swear to uphold and protect the woolly principles . . . ' " Jane was laughing too hard to finish.

Shelley drew herself up. "Nice women don't snort like that when they're talking, Jane."

"You'll have to warn Edgar off serving mutton," Jane said, and went off into another laughing fit. "I wonder if any of your club members are 'on the lamb.'"

Shelley looked to heaven for guidance.

# —— 2 ——

On Tuesday afternoon the week the reunion was to start, Jane went to the Francisco mansion with Shelley to meet Edgar North and familiarize herself with the layout of the house and her responsibilities.

The house had a definitely Gothic look. The three-acre lot was surrounded by a tall filigree iron fence, freshly painted with glossy black paint. "It looks like an English mental institution from the turn of the century," Jane commented to Shelley as they passed through the gates. The mansion was truly a mansion, with turrets, towers, and misguided bits of iron railings around the roof edges and dormers. Tall pines and oaks, showing scars of recent cosmetic trimming, still darkened the overall gloomy aspect, which was not helped by the fact that a dank fall drizzle was falling.

"I've seen this place from the road, but I've never been in here," Jane said. "I thought it was abandoned."

"The Francisco family moved out the year Ted died and it was vacant until Edgar and Gordon bought it last January," Shelley replied as she wheeled her van into a parking spot by the carriage house behind the main house.

"So Ted died," Jane mused.

Shelley looked at her, perplexed, then said, "Sorry. I'm in my reunion mode. I forgot you haven't always lived in this neighborhood."

"Who the hell is Ted? The resident ghost?"

"Dear God! I hope not! I'll tell you about it later. There's Edgar waving at us."

They got out of the car and went to the back door. A cherubic man in his early fifties with thinning red hair, a hint of potbelly, and a huge smile was holding the storm door open to them. "Ghastly weather, isn't it? I hope it clears up for your guests. Come in, ladies," he said, beaming.

Jane stepped into the kitchen and came to a dead stop. Nothing could have been more in contrast to the outer aspect of the house. The kitchen was huge, brightly lighted, and seemed to hum with warmth and welcome. Gleaming copper pans, ladles, strainers, and baskets were hung from the soffit around the room. A big kitchen table by the windows was draped in a bright calico fabric that matched the ruffled curtains next to it. White tile counters reflected the bright lighting; a huge, bleached butcher block workstation was in the center of the room. The most gigantic refrigerator Jane had ever seen dominated the far end of the room and white, glass-fronted cabinets held arrays of china and sparkling crystal. There was a quarry tile floor with colorful rag rugs placed anywhere a person might stand for a few moments.

"Mr. North, this is the kitchen of my dreams!" Jane said reverently. "Heaven looks just like this."

"Darling, it's Edgar. *Mr.* North is my father in Cleveland. And I'm glad you like it. I'm rather pleased myself."

"You could store a small northern country in that refrigerator. But this is a bed and breakfast. Surely—"

"Surely I don't need this to throw together a bit of eggs and toast?" Edgar finished for her. "No, but I'm a chef by profession. I've worked all over the country. And this is the kitchen I've always wanted for myself when it came time to settle down. We're going to do dinners, as well, you see. Not like a restaurant, just for planned parties. Maybe some catering when we're better established. Now sit down, my dears, and let me give you some coffee."

"Coffee" turned out to be a divine concoction that tasted so nutty and rich that Jane didn't see how she'd ever go back to the ordinary kind. Along with it Edgar served the tiniest, most delicate cream puffs on earth. Jane and Shelley complimented him effusively between bites. "Aren't you having any of your own marvelous treats?" Jane asked, wondering if Shelley would slap her hand if she took a fourth cream puff. She decided to risk it.

"No, have to watch my tummy," Edgar said, patting his tidy little potbelly.

"BRBRBROEWW!" someone said from the next room. A second later an enormous, sleek Siamese cat sauntered into the room

"What a handsome cat!" Jane exclaimed.

Shelley looked at her as if she'd lost a considerable number of brain cells.

"His name is Hector. The noun and the verb," Edgar said. "He's supposed to be outside mousing to earn his keep, but he hates the rain."

Hector came over and rammed his head into Jane's leg, then flopped down and rolled over as if indicating that this luscious furry expanse of stomach he was exposing just might be available for petting. Jane obliged.

"Are you ready to take a look around? I'm sorry Gordon isn't here to help me show off. He's responsible for all the decorating. I'm just the cook."

"The understatement of the year," Jane said, licking powdered sugar off her fingertips and realizing too late there was a bit of cat fur sticking to them as well.

"Where is Gordon?" Shelley asked.

"Still holding down gainful employment. He's design production coordinator for a greeting card company in Chicago. Dreadful job, of course. All cute little bunny wabbits and cripplingly sweet verse, but it keeps the wolf from the door. We're hoping that we'll rake in such pots of cash that he can quit when we get running."

The tour of the house left Jane gasping. Each guest bedroom had a name that matched its decor. The sunflower room, the apricot room, the moonlight room, the cornflower room, the tuxedo room, the lime room, the rose room. Bedspreads, curtains, carpet, paintings, lampshades were all exquisitely coordinated. The rose room was a symphony of femininity, all blushing cabbage roses, cherrywood, and quilting, while the moonlight room was as cool, classical, and masculine as Cary Grant. Hector preceded them into each room as if he were personally responsible for the decor. Every now and then he let out a spine-tingling Siamese yowl that made Shelley shudder and Jane giggle. Edgar kept giving the cat indulgent, fatherly looks.

"I want to adopt Gordon," Jane said. "Do you two have rooms here or in the carriage house?"

"We have what we laughingly call a 'suite' on the third floor right now," Edgar answered. "Nasty place. Meant for stunted midget maids. Gordon's head is perpetually black-and-blue from crashing into the ceiling where it takes weird dives. We suspect bats, but the lighting is so poor we're not sure. We're probably going to live in the carriage house eventually, but right now it's just for storage. And for mice, which Gordon claims Hector is afraid of."

"Then nobody will have a room there. Good," Shelley said. At Jane and Edgar's questioning looks, she added cryptically, "Bad vibes. Especially for this group."

Edgar showed them around the ground floor rooms: a vast formal dining room, a living room with game tables, sofa groupings, and a sound and video system that would have made Jane's son Mike weep with envy. There was even a Nintendo game hooked up. "That's for guests with children," Edgar explained a little too hastily.

"I thought you didn't take children?" Jane said.

"Well, no—we don't plan to, but—"

Jane grinned broadly. "You're an addict. I know the signs. What's your favorite? Mine's Chrysalis."

Edgar actually blushed to the roots of his fine hair. "Actually, I like the maze kinds best. Lolo, that sort."

Shelley stared at the two of them, aghast. "You play those games?"

"Someday I'll get you hooked," Jane threatened. "Is this the library?" She glanced into a darkened room next to the living room.

Edgar went in and turned on the lights. It was the perfect library—three walls of dark oak bookshelves, a long library table with green-shaded lamps, chairs and sofas of soft, comfortable leather, and an oak library ladder that slid along one wall. There was even a fax machine and a copy machine ready for businessmen and women who couldn't, or wouldn't, leave their work behind.

Jane went to a shelf of paperbacks with matching orange spines. "P. G. Wodehouse! Are these yours? Edgar, I think I'll adopt you instead of Gordon. 'There is only one real cure for gray hair. It was invented by a Frenchman. He called it the guillotine,' " Jane quoted.

" 'The magistrate looked like an owl with a dash of weasel blood in him,' " Edgar came back.

They were laughing happily and tossing quotes back and forth when they became aware of Shelley tapping her foot and clearing her throat ominously at intervals.

"Yes, all right," Jane said. "Edgar, you better tell me what to do and show me where the skivvy stuff is."

They toured the broom and vacuum cleaner closet and the linen closets, then Edgar said, "Now come out to the carriage house. The rags are there."

"A whole house, just for rags?" Jane asked as they hurried through the drizzle across the driveway and into the carriage house through the ground floor garage doors. Hector sensibly remained behind in the warm, dry house. There was, his expression suggested, a limit to what one would do for guests.

There was a jumbled heap of fabric in the middle of the floor. "These, ladies, were all the old rotten curtains and drapes in the house. I took out the hardware, washed them, and threw them in here to turn into rags as I need them. All the yard stuff's here, too, and extra cleaning supplies. I got a by-the-crate bargain on bathroom cleaner and dishwasher soap and over there is a mountain of toilet paper." He pointed into the gloom at the back of the triple garage.

"Is there more stuff upstairs here?" Jane asked.

"No, we haven't done anything to that yet. It's a relic of a boy's room. Sort of poignant, really—that the people left it. Posters, football trophies, a battered desk with school homework papers still in the drawers.

# —— 3 ——

ᵥednesday morning was wildly hectic. Jane's caɪ ᵊl schedule—as elaborate as a schedule of Mafia ᵗs, her Uncle Jim claimed—fell to pieces. The ᵗher who was supposed to drive Jane's high school ɪ Mike's car pool called sounding like she was iɪ ᵉ final stages of pneumonia and tried to get Jane tᴐ ᵗe her place.

"I'm sorry, but I've got the grade school this week ᵈ the whole junior high group has come down with ᵐething and I've got to drive my daughter, too. I'm ally sorry, but you'll just have to press your husband ₐto service," Jane said firmly. She probably would ᵥve caved in and helped if it had been humanly ᵊssible. It would have put the other driver under a ᵉrrific obligation. Being owed a car pool favor wasn't ᴐ be taken lightly.

"Oh, Jane, you know what an idiot Stan is about ᵗar pools."

"Stan runs a whole bank! He's just convinced you ᵥe's too stupid to figure out how to drive the kids so you won't ask him to help," Jane said. "It's selective idiocy. Steve used to do the same thing."

There was some more sniffling and whining at the other end. Jane sympathized. Her own late husband Steve, who had died in a car accident a year and a half earlier, had been just as discriminately parental.

Sort of chokes you up to think of pitching it all."

"That's Ted's room," Shelley said.

"Dead Ted?" Jane asked.

"Dead Ted! That sounds like a rock group," Edgar said, laughing uneasily.

"Ted Francisco," Shelley said. "I guess I better explain to both of you—just in case anything awkward happens."

"Are you anticipating 'something awkward'?" Jane asked.

Edgar looked distinctly unhappy at this turn in the conversation.

Shelley didn't answer directly. "This house belonged to Judge Francisco. He and his wife had a son Ted, who was in our class in high school. He was handsome, smart, athletic, everything. We were all madly in love with him. He had everything going for him." She paused for a moment before finishing. "The night of our senior prom, he committed suicide."

"Where?" Edgar asked quietly.

Shelley pointed above them. "In that room."

"Another cream puff?" Edgar asked Jane solicitously. They were back in the bright, cheerful kitchen. Hector was lashing himself against Jane's legs.

"My thighs will have to have their own zip code if I eat another," Jane said. She turned to Shelley. "How did he do it? Dead Ted, I mean."

"Carbon monoxide. Besides the stairway upstairs, there's a sort of hatch at the back of the garage. It opened next to Ted's bed. It used to be a joke with us. Ted could be out of there as fast as a fireman, flinging up the hatch, sliding down a rope almost into the front seat of his car. Anyway, that night he left the car running and the hatch open. His parents were out of town overnight and when they came back, they found him fully dressed in bed. Dead. It was horrible for them. He was literally the light of their lives. An only child, born to them when they were in their late forties, I believe. Judge Francisco had a complete breakdown. By the time he recovered, his wife had closed the house and they moved away. I didn't realize they'd left Ted's room just like it was. I guess they couldn't stand to get rid of his things and just walked away and left it."

"Do you think this is why the house was vacant for so long?" Edgar asked. "We bought it from their estate."

"My guess is that they couldn't make themselves come back to the house, but couldn't bear to sell it either," Shelley said. "So they're both dead. Not surprising. They were a much older couple than the rest of our parents. They had Ted very late in life."

"It's a shame the house was left to stand vacant so long. It's a lovely place," Jane said.

"It wasn't so lovely when we got it," Edgar said. "In fact, I wouldn't have gone along with buying it if Gordon hadn't been so confident that something could be made of it. There had been transients living here off and on and the police told us—after we bought it, of course—that a drug ring had been operating out of here. Why, some of the riffraff have even turned up since we moved in. One night, we heard scrabbling noises and came down to find a young couple in what you might call 'a delicate situation' right in the middle of the living room. Thrashing around in a pile of sawdust. That's why we're awfully fussy about keeping the doors locked at night. We're going to ask guests to be in by ten-thirty or they'll have to wake us to get in."

"There must be a lot of details to work out when you're opening a place like this," Jane

"Probably a lot more that we haven't of yet. But your group will be a nice trial I'm sure it's going to go wonderfully wel with determined brightness.

Jane was surprised that Shelley didn't continued to stare out the window at th was frowning. It was always a bad sign w frowned. "I hope I haven't made a big m said, more to herself than to them.

Jane hung up on the other mother and screamed up the stairs, "Katie! Hurry up!"

"I'm doing my hair!" came back the indignant reply.

"You better get a move on. I've got to take you early so I can get Todd's gang picked up."

As Jane rounded up kids, helped hunt for lost math homework, and emptied her purse for lunch money, she reflected on how shortsighted she'd been to allow her children to be spaced out in such a way that they attended three different schools. Why couldn't she have just had triplets and been done with it? Everybody would have done everything at the same time— started school, lost baby teeth, gotten hormones. There would have been brief periods of absolute hell, but they'd have never been repeated with the next kid.

It was a bright sunny day out when she headed toward school with Katie, and the early morning light was catching the tops of trees just starting to show hints of vivid fall coloration. "Oh, look at that one!" Jane said, pointing toward an especially gorgeous scarlet ivy climbing a chimney.

"Don't turn this way!" Katie shrieked.

"Why not? It's the way to school," Jane asked.

"Mom, Jenny lives on this street!"

"Of course she does." Jenny was Katie's best friend.

Katie was scrunching down in the seat, squealing protests. "She'll see me! Why couldn't you go some other way?"

"Katie, Jenny's whole family has the flu; I doubt very much that Jenny's been up since dawn peering out the window to see if we go by and what difference would it make if she had? Have you and Jenny had a tiff?"

"Mom, don't use words like that. They're so lame."

"Tiff is a perfectly good word. So have you had a spat, quarrel, rumble, confrontation, take your choice." The silence that met this inquiry answered it. "What was it about, honey?"

"You wouldn't understand," Katie grumbled. She'd crawled back up to a vertical position and was craned around, looking back at Jenny's house.

"Try me," Jane said.

Katie just sniffed pitifully, begging to be begged.

Jane dutifully begged.

Finally, just as they turned the last corner and the school loomed up in front of them, Katie relented. "Mom, she *told* Jason I liked him."

Jane tried to cast her mind back and appreciate the gravity of this treason. "Why would she do that?"

"She's mad at me. There's this new girl at school she likes better than me and I said she was fat. Well, Mom, she is!"

Jane sorted through the pronouns, assigning them, and came to the conclusion that the new girl was the fat one. Jenny herself was a bit plump, but Jane didn't think Katie even noticed that anymore. There were a thousand true, sensible and "motherly" things to say to her daughter, but Jane knew Katie didn't want to hear them and it would slam the door on further confidences. "I think the best thing is to act like you don't care," she ventured. "Jenny will remember pretty soon that you're her best friend and she'll be sorry she told Jason."

All her careful selection of words went for nothing. Katie wasn't paying any attention. As Jane stopped the car in the circle drive in front of the school, Katie put the back of her hand to her forehead. "I think I'm getting sick. You better take me back home."

"No way, kiddo." But just the same, she felt Katie's

forehead. "They'd all think you were afraid to come to school if you stayed out today. Besides, I'm going to be gone all day."

It was the wrong thing to say . . . again. "Mom! Why do you have to treat me like such a baby. I could stay home by myself."

Jane remembered Staying Home By Myself from her own school days. "No deal. Hop out."

The phone was ringing when Jane came back in the door to her kitchen after delivering the grade schoolers. It was Detective Mel VanDyne, the man she was dating in an extremely sporadic fashion. "Jane? I'm glad I caught you. Listen, about Saturday night . . ."

"You're canceling."

"Sorry, but I've got to. It's a follow-up to that drugs in the schools seminar I taught last week. It seems that . . ."

"It's all right," Jane said, even though it wasn't. She'd bought a new outfit.

"How about Sunday night instead?"

"Sorry. I'm busy."

There was a silence Jane hoped wasn't patently disbelieving. Well, she *was* busy on Sunday night. All Sunday nights, in fact. There was always at least one child who had to have help on a report that had been assigned a week earlier, another who couldn't find a precious article of clothing he/she *had* to wear the next day, and one who decided to practice some musical instrument next to the phone that a sibling was speaking on. It was that way every school night, but for some mysterious reason Sundays were always the worst. Not that she had any intention of letting a sophisticated bachelor know what sort of things she was busy with. She'd been dating Mel off and on

(more off than on, to her regret) for two months
and he was still wary of her extraordinarily maternal
life-style. He always seemed half-afraid she was going
to lose her head and pack him a lunch or drive him to
a piano lesson.

"If it weren't my own class—" Mel finally said.

"No, don't explain. I didn't mean to sound snappish.
I'm just a little rushed. I'm on my way to the airport in
a few minutes and I always have to sort of 'commune
with my soul' before I tackle the drive."

"You're having visitors?"

"No, Shelley is. A class reunion. I've been drafted
to help with the convoy."

"How about tonight for the dinner and movie then?
You'll deserve it."

"I do hate to keep turning you down, but I really
can't tonight." (Oops, did that "really" give away the
earlier lie, she wondered.) "Shelley's got me booked—
or hooked. Any night next week, though. How about
Tuesday?"

Mel agreed that Tuesday fit his schedule, too. This
settled, they rang off and Jane poured herself a thermal
mug of coffee to take along. With any luck she'd be
at the airport a good half hour before anybody arrived.
This would allow her to make the drive without wor-
rying about the clock and give her time to get her
bearings. The three women she was supposed to pick
up were coming in on three different flights and she
would have to know where she was going next to keep
from missing them.

She put on a black-and-white plaid skirt and her
good black sweater, freshly out of summer storage. It
was a good thing it was unusually cool for September.
Jane was sick to death of her summer clothes. She
hastily applied some makeup, glanced once more at

the city map to refresh her memory, and went out to the car.

During the interval while Jane had been inside the house, Shelley had put something on the front seat of her station wagon. Three modest-sized posterboards with a name on each: Lila Switzer, Susan Morgan, and Avalon Smith. And on the back of each, as a reminder, the airline, flight number, and arrival time of each.

Trust Shelley to be so organized.

It was a good thing Jane had allowed herself extra time. She missed bullying her way into the correct exit lane and had to go to the next exit and backtrack. Fortunately she had better luck parking and made it into the airport well ahead of the first flight she was due to meet.

If only she had some idea whom to look for. She was going to feel a bit silly holding up a placard. She'd asked Shelley for descriptions of the women she was meeting, but Shelley had refused to help. "Jane, it's been twenty years since I've seen them. God only knows what they all look like by now. I'll fix it so they find you."

The first flight was actually a bit early and Jane dutifully held up her "Susan Morgan" placard as the passengers flowed from the door to the walkway.

"Why, hello. Who are you?" an attractively coiffed and tanned woman said to her.

"I'm Jane Jeffry, Shelley's neighbor. Are you Ms. Morgan?"

The woman put a hand with expensively sculpted nails and a number of exceedingly expensive rings on Jane's arm. "This year I am. Next year, who knows? And please, none of that 'Ms.' stuff. Just call me Crispy. Everybody else at the reunion will."

"They will?" Jane asked, smiling. "Why on earth would they do a thing like that?"

The woman laughed warmly. "Because my maiden name, back in the dark days of my maidenhood, was Susan Crisp. I like you, Jane. I might make you my assistant."

"Assistant what?"

"Tormentor. Oh, this is going to be *such* fun." She rubbed her lovely hands together like a stage villain. "I can't wait to see everybody. I've got about a dozen bags and my hairdresser is crammed into one of them. Where shall I meet you?"

"My next gate is around the turn down there, first on the left, and the next is at the far end of the same concourse. Can you manage the bags?"

"My dear, I can manage anything." And she sounded as if she could. She went off chuckling to herself. Jane watched her go with a mixture of amusement and alarm. Assistant tormentor? Good God, what had Shelley let herself in for?

*More important, what has she let me in for?*

As if feeling Jane's eyes on her, Crispy—halfway down the concourse and drawing a number of admiring looks—turned gracefully on a spiked, lizard-skinned heel, waggled her fingers, and winked conspiratorially.

The last time Jane had seen an expression like that was when her sister Martha had decided to purchase a high school term paper and blackmailed Jane into being her go-between. Jane's father had caught her slinking out of the house with the cash wadded in her fist. If she recalled correctly, as she was certain she did, Jane herself had gotten the entire blame for the episode.

# ─── 4 ───

The next one Jane was to meet didn't have half
the exuberance of Crispy. Avalon Smith looked like
a well-preserved "flower child" with the careless wad
of burgundy-red hair, freshly scrubbed, makeup-free
face, and layers of droopy, no-special-color clothing. She had a long brown scarf flung around her
neck, and an equally nondescript necklace made of
wood and bits of something that looked like varnished
dirt clods.

"I'm Avalon Smith," she almost whispered to Jane,
as if admitting to a rather embarrassing secret.

Jane introduced herself. "If you want to get your
bags and come back here, I'll fetch you when I've
met one more person."

"I just have this," Avalon said, indicating a big,
squashy tapestry bag that had been indistinguishable
from her garb.

"Then come along."

Avalon trailed along as obediently as an eccentrical-
ly clad carnival pony. "Did you have a good flight?"
Jane asked.

"Oh, yes."

That was it. Jane waited for polite elaboration, but
there wasn't any. "Where did you come from?" Jane
asked, feeling obligated to make conversation.

"Arkansas."

Jane wanted to grab Avalon's arm (if she could find it in all that organic clothing) and say, "Look at me when you talk!" but she didn't.

They settled themselves at the last gate and Jane looked desperately at her watch. Only ten minutes to wait. Unless—God Forbid!—the plane was late! "So . . . are you excited about seeing all your old friends from school?" Jane asked.

Avalon thought hard. "I guess so."

Jane was spared any further attempts at chitchat by Crispy's arrival. This amazing woman had managed to snag one of the overgrown go-carts that ferry infirm passengers around. It was piled high with a half dozen pieces of matched luggage that looked like they were made of periwinkle blue suede. Jane had never seen anything like it outside of an expensive catalog display. The cart was driven by a good-looking young man who was smiling as if he'd been given a stupendous tip. "I've twisted my ankle, haven't I, Derek?" Crispy said, grinning.

Then she spotted Avalon and leaped off the cart. "Avalon Delvecchio! Imagine! After all these years!" She enveloped Avalon, limp as a rag doll, in a fierce embrace.

"I'm sorry—I don't—" Avalon mumbled.

"You don't know who I am, do you, dear!" Crispy crowed. She glanced at Jane for confirmation, then back to Avalon. "It's me. Crispy."

"Crispy! It can't be. You're so—" She stopped, appalled at what she'd been about to say.

Crispy said it for her. "Thin, pretty, rich? Isn't it amazing?" She whirled around to let Avalon get a better look, then explained to Jane. "I was the fat, pimpled slob with the nibbled nails and terrible hair.

Isn't it amazing what marrying three or four rich men can do for a girl?"

"You've been married that many times?" Avalon asked.

"Oh, at least. That was just the rich ones. My darling Avalon, I'd have known you anywhere. You look exactly the same. You must have a gallon of formaldehyde for breakfast every day. What's your name now?"

"Smith," Avalon said, still in shock and acting like she wasn't sure she believed this was who she said she was.

"What a pity. Still, we can't have everything. Why, I married Landsdale Brooke-Trevor just for his name and he turned out to be an impotent pansy. You see what I mean?"

"I—I think so."

"Who are we waiting for?" Crispy said to Jane.

"Oh, the plane's here, isn't it!" Jane said with surprise and hastily scrambled to find her placard. "This flight is Lila Switzer."

"Dear Delilah . . ." Crispy cooed maliciously. "No, don't hold that thing up. I'll know her, but she won't know me."

Crispy watched as disembarking passengers passed them. As she got ready to pounce, a severely well-dressed woman with a glossy twist of fair hair turned and said, "Well, Crispy. Imagine seeing you here. And Avalon. How nice." This couldn't have been frostier if she'd had a mouthful of dry ice.

Crispy was crestfallen. "You recognized me?"

"Well, of course. You haven't changed a bit."

Crispy stared at her for a moment, then took a deep breath and said, "I see."

Challenge delivered.

And returned.

Jane leaped in and explained her own role in their meeting. "We're *all* staying at Shelley's house?" Lila asked coolly.

"No, at a bed and breakfast nearby," Jane said, feeling vaguely as though she'd been chided. "They aren't open yet, officially, and Shelley arranged—"

"Quite." Lila cut her off.

"Do you have bags?"

"Only my garment bag," Lila said, indicating the object she was holding over her left arm. In her right hand she had a briefcase and a large, expensive but dowdy handbag. Jane had been studying her and suddenly realized what was so odd about her appearance. Everything she wore or carried looked like it once belonged to a great aunt. Jane's mother had a friend like that, an old "pillar of Boston," who said everything should be looked upon as an investment for your grandchildren. "Buy the very best quality, take excellent care of it, and hand it on to another generation," Jane had once heard the woman say. The old lady actually got extra fabric when each of her suits was made and had it cleaned with the suit so that it would match when it was needed to make alterations for another decade's—or generation's—use.

Lila Switzer's suit could have been purchased during World War II at tremendous expense and cleaned and altered over half a century—and still looked good. The same could be said for her shoes, briefcase, handbag, and perfect old-fashioned hair. *She's wearing Grace Kelly's hair!* Jane thought to herself.

"So you're Shelley's neighbor," Crispy said.

"Yes, for years now." Jane was relieved that no

one had spoken to her until she got back into familiar territory. She wasn't good at highway driving and chatting at the same time. They hadn't even talked much to each other. Avalon rode in front with Jane and hadn't said a word. She'd hauled some knitting needles and mouse brown hairy yarn out of one of her bags as soon as they got to the car and clicked the needles all the way. In the backseat, Crispy and Lila, apparently in a state of uneasy truce, sporadically compared notes on some classmates. Who'd married, divorced, had interesting operations.

"Are you married?" Crispy asked, tapping Jane on the shoulder.

"Widowed," Jane answered.

"Oh, God! I've never had any of mine die on me!" Crispy said. "How awful for you. I'm so sorry I asked."

"Don't be," Jane said pleasantly. "Your asking didn't make it happen. And it's more or less okay that it did."

"Who else is coming to this meeting?" Lila demanded, apparently feeling that talk of death was gauche. Or perhaps she was merely bored with a conversation that had nothing to do with her.

"I'm sorry. The names didn't mean much to me and I'm afraid I don't remember," Jane answered. "Somebody named Mimi, I think, and a person Shelley refers to as 'Pooky.' And I think there's one or two more."

"Pooky's coming?" Crispy asked. "Then get all your insecurities mustered and ready for action."

"Why's that?" Jane asked.

"Because she's so beautiful you'll feel like half a dozen ugly stepsisters."

"Some were coming by train," Jane explained. "Shelley picked them up."

"Oh, look! That little park is still there," Crispy said from the backseat. "Look, Lila. Didn't you live over there someplace? Which was your house? I don't remember."

"The green one. Only it was tan then," Lila answered.

Jane turned the last corner.

"Why, this is my block!" Crispy said. "Remember? The house right . . ." Her voice trailed off as Jane drove through the gates of the Francisco mansion.

"Good God!" Avalon exclaimed. "This is Ted Francisco's house!"

Jane was so surprised at the vehemence of Avalon's remark that she spoke somewhat sharply. "Not anymore. It's a bed and breakfast belonging to Edgar and Gordon. You'll be bowled over by Edgar's cooking. And Gordon has redecorated the house magnificently. They even have a resident cat, Hector, who's a love." She wasn't going to allow any Dead Ted talk.

Instead of going to the driveway by the back door, Jane pulled up the circle drive and stopped at the front door. As her passengers began to get out and sort through their luggage and miscellaneous belongings, the door opened and Shelley said, "Oh, look who's here."

Two other women joined her in the doorway. Then there were shrieks of greeting and a lot of really insincere hugging and complimenting. But there was also some genuine warmth in their greetings and Jane felt herself just a little jealous of this kind of old-fashioned camaraderie between old friends. Most of these women had grown up together in the days before people routinely moved every couple of years. Some had probably been friends, or at least acquaintances, for the first half of their lives.

After the first round of greetings had died down, Shelley introduced Jane. "This is my neighbor, Jane Jeffry, who is helping Edgar and me. Jane, this is Mimi Soong."

Jane shook hands with the elegant Chinese woman. "It's very nice of you to get involved in this," Mimi said. "She must really have something on you," she added with a lovely smile.

"And this is Debbie Poole, but you might as well know her as Pooky," Shelley added. There was a note of warning in her voice that was nearly frantic.

Jane could see why. Shelley and Crispy had both mentioned how astoundingly beautiful Pooky was, but Pooky in the flesh was a mess. Her skin was leathery and so wrinkled that it looked like a bizarre medical condition. Here and there it pulled as if she'd had plastic surgery in somebody's basement as an experiment. Her hair was bleached to the point of fragility. It looked as if it would shatter if touched. She was excruciatingly thin and almost painfully well-dressed. Jane suspected most of her clothes still had their sale tags lurking nearby.

"How do you do, Pooky," Jane said heartily. Even though Jane had never seen the woman before, she found her appearance very nearly shocking. The others were frankly dumbfounded and were now standing in a rough semicircle studying Pooky with silent horror and a good deal of genuine sadness.

*Poor woman,* Jane thought. "Crispy has brought enough luggage to stay a year and a half. Or maybe she's opening a dress shop," she said firmly to the group. "I'm afraid we're all going to have to pitch in and help carry it."

As she'd hoped, that broke the spell. There was a babble of embarrassed conversation as Jane opened the back door of her station wagon and started handing out bag after matched bag. Jane and Mimi Soong ended up with the last pieces. Hector had appeared and was daintily exploring the interior of Jane's station wagon.

"You handled that very well," Mimi said.

"I felt so sorry for her. Everybody staring."

"She'd been telling Shelley and me about it when you arrived," Mimi said, hanging back so she wouldn't be overheard. "She had some kind of treatment. It was supposed to preserve her youthful looks forever. You wouldn't think anybody'd be stupid enough to buy that, but she was. Brains aren't her long suit. It went horribly wrong, as you can see, and apparently she won a big lawsuit against the outfit that did it to her. But the money couldn't restore her looks. It's a pity. She really was beautiful. And like many beautiful people, she didn't develop any backup. Brains or personality or anything."

"That's terrible. Poor thing."

Mimi laughed. "You'll get over being so sad about it when you've been around her a while. She's quite irritating. Her voice alone will glue your heart back together. I'm sorry. I shouldn't be saying that. She's really a thoroughly nice woman. I can carry another bag. Give me that hatbox-shaped thing."

Jane stared into the back of the station wagon. "My God, I haven't seen a hatbox since the last time I played in my grandmother's attic."

"Attic . . ." Mimi said. "I think that's the operative word. By the time this is over, you're going to feel like you've spent the week in somebody else's attic. Does it look to you like that cat is getting ready to drive your car away?"

Hector was standing with his front feet on the steering wheel, peering over the dashboard. His Godiva-chocolate ears were flattened to his head as if he were ready to have a crash helmet fitted.

## 5

Jane left them to their greetings and went home—
after gently putting Hector out of the car. She shoved
him in the front door for good measure, to be sure
she didn't run over him. She was off duty until three,
when she had to return and help Edgar with dinner
preparations. It wasn't that he needed her, but she saw
it as an opportunity to get to watch a really good cook
in action. The kids had been complaining lately about
having the same stuff over and over again for dinners.
Maybe she could freshen up her repertoire.

She lined up several loads of laundry, fielded a
couple of phone calls wanting her to contribute to
charities, buy siding, and take out a new credit card,
and then she went down to her office in the basement
to work on her book. Some months earlier her mother
had come to visit and had wanted to take a course in
writing an autobiography. Jane, not wanting to write
her own, had made up a fictional person to write about
and the teacher had encouraged her to continue. Jane
wasn't sure it was even a real novel, or if it would
ever leave her basement, but she was enjoying the
experience enormously. Most of the time.

But today she found it hard to concentrate. Her
mind kept going back to Shelley's classmates. She had
dreaded this because she thought it would be so dull.
But they hadn't proved dull at all. Scary, rather. All

those emotions, presumably tucked away for years, boiling to the surface. But that wasn't fair. Some of them had seemed truly glad to see one another. When she left, Pooky and Avalon were deep in an animated discussion on the front porch. At least those two would enjoy catching up on the missing years. And perhaps others of them would have fun, too. Jane realized she was putting too much of her own spin on this reunion.

She plowed on with writing and laundry and three o'clock finally came. She'd put a casserole in the fridge with instructions to the children as to when to put it in the oven. There were chips out on the table and a saucepan with green beans (the only vegetable they all liked) sitting on top of the casserole, where it couldn't be missed. They'd probably have sodas with their meal instead of the milk she kept forcing on them, but it wouldn't kill them.

When she returned to the bed and breakfast, the other two members of the group had apparently just arrived. There was luggage in the front hallway and greetings were going on all over again.

She was introduced to Beth Vaughn and Shelley's *précis* came back to her. "She's a judge. Our class's most successful graduate. She's expected to be a Supreme Court nominee next time they decide it's trendy to put another woman on the court," Shelley had said. Beth Vaughn certainly looked the part. She had crisply curling, no-nonsense graying hair, cut very short. Her blue suit and white blouse were neat and sensible, as were her low-heeled shoes. She might have had a good figure, but the suit de-emphasized it, giving her a square, sexless look. Her manner was pleasant, but reserved. She had very pretty eyes, which was the only thing that kept her looking feminine.

"It's very generous of you to give up your time to help Shelley and us," she said graciously. "I hope you don't find it too boring to be marooned in among strangers."

"I'm quite used to it," Jane said, inadvertently adopting Beth's formal tone. "I was a State Department brat."

"How very interesting that must have been," Beth said warmly. "I've always regretted that I didn't have more opportunities to travel. Perhaps you can tell me more later about the places you've lived."

"And who's this? I don't recognize you at all?"

Another woman had joined them and Beth Vaughn drifted away.

"I'm not one of you," Jane said to the strange woman. "I'm Shelley's friend Jane. I'm just helping Edgar. This place isn't supposed to be open for business yet and he hasn't hired help—so I'm the help," Jane said.

"God! What a dreary thing for you! I'm Kathy Herrmannson, what was Emerson back in the old days."

This one was a mess, too. But unlike poor Pooky, who got that way trying too hard to preserve her looks, Kathy apparently never gave her appearance a thought. She was overweight in a particularly sloppy, hippy way, which was made worse by her bulgy jeans and unflattering T-shirt. Jane was reminded of one of the advice maven's words: if you can put a pencil under you breast and it stays there, you shouldn't go braless. Kathy could have tucked away a wrench. The unpleasantly distorted T-shirt was emblazoned with a faded peace symbol. Her face was pasty and free of any makeup, which was unfortunate.

"I'm glad to meet you, Kathy," Jane said.

"Does the cook know I don't eat meat?" Kathy asked.

"I have no idea. I'll go ask," Jane said, glad to escape.

She went into Edgar's beautiful kitchen and found him mincing shallots. Hector was sitting on a kitchen chair, supervising. "Do you know you've got a vegetarian out there?" Jane asked.

He shrugged. "No problem. She can just eat around the meat. I'm fixing creamed chicken in puff pastry shells and peas with nutmeg. And some old-fashioned deviled eggs. She's not one of those full-fledged no-animal-products people, is she?"

"I don't think so. It looks like she exists on macaroni and chocolates."

"Oh, the fleshy one. I noticed her. She must live in a house without mirrors. Jane, get some butter for me, would you? I need it clarified."

When Edgar figured out that Jane had no idea how to clarify butter, at least not to his standards, he suggested that she join the guests. "Just keep an eye on the snack tray. If it runs low, refill it. Refresh drinks, that sort of thing."

The women had divided up into little groups, with everybody trying to listen to everybody else's conversations. Jane approached Avalon and Mimi, who were studying a sheet of paper. Avalon's red topknot had come loose and was falling around her face, like a curtain to hide behind. She was mumbling shy thanks. Mimi looked even more serene compared to Avalon. Mimi's straight black hair, for all the hugging, looked like the lacquered hair of an exquisite Chinese doll.

"May I get you ladies something to drink?" Jane asked.

Mimi shook her head and gently took the paper from Avalon. "Jane, look at this lovely sketch Avalon brought along."

It was an incredibly busy pencil drawing. "It's the carriage house here, isn't it?" Jane said. "How lovely."

"Look at the detail," Mimi instructed.

As Jane studied the picture, she started to smile. It was full of quiet little jokes. The bush beside the coach house wasn't just squiggly lines as it first appeared, it was a seething mass of tiny rabbits. Bricks had faces hidden in them. So did tree trunks. A few random rocks along the drive were actually a chorus line of raccoons. There was a peddler with his pack in a cloud and a witch hidden in the branches of a tree.

"This is delightful!" Jane exclaimed. "You must show it to Edgar. He'll love it!"

"Do you think so?" Avalon whispered.

Pooky came over to take a look and went hysterical with enthusiasm. "Why, this is wonderful. I love it! Oh, Avalon, would you consider giving it to me? I have just the perfect place to hang it in my apartment. It would change the whole room and mean all the more because an old friend made it."

Kathy slouched by, her mouth full of ham and egg roll. "Hey, Avalon, that's cute," she said, spitting a few crumbs as she spoke. "Have you ever used this talent of yours for anything worthwhile?"

"Worthwhile?" Mimi asked with a dangerous smile.

"Socially worthwhile. We all owe it to society to use our gifts to benefit mankind," Kathy said.

"Oh, put a sock in it," Crispy said cheerfully from across the room. Several others laughed. "Avalon doesn't owe anybody anything, Kathy. And if she did go crusading, she might not crusade for *your* causes. Have you thought about that? Just what are your causes these days, anyway?"

She'd said it in a light, joking way, but Kathy, though not the least offended, took it to be a serious question. "The same as always, Crispy. Peace, love, the protection of the environment. . . ."

The individual groups fell silent as Crispy snapped, "Oh, come on! That's all so easy and trendy to say. What are you doing about any of it?"

"As much as we can," Kathy said smugly. She took a deep breath and several people decently averted their eyes from the expanding T-shirt. "My husband and children and I drive into Tulsa and volunteer every Saturday at the local recycling center. I make my own soap—"

"All it takes is piss and ashes," someone muttered. Jane glanced around but nobody looked guilty.

"No, it takes time and love and dedication," Kathy said. Her voice suddenly caught in something between a hiccup and a snort.

Pooky had ignored the whole controversy and was still begging for the picture. Avalon didn't seem to know how to say no to her, but hadn't turned loose of it yet.

"It's a lovely drawing, Avalon," Jane said, getting the conversation back on what she hoped was a less dangerous course. Avalon's next words dispelled this happy notion.

"I did it the night of the prom," Avalon said.

A sort of collective shudder went around the room.

"The night Ted died?" Crispy asked softly, although they all knew the answer.

Avalon looked as if she were remembering a dream that was both wonderful and horrible. "Yes, there was moonlight almost as bright as day. I'd just finished it when I heard the car engine start and I thought he would back out any minute and catch me drawing the house, so I ran away."

The words hung in the air. They all knew Ted hadn't backed his car out, but had gone back upstairs to die.

Pooky hadn't given up trying to acquire the drawing. "It's so wonderful!"

Jane was casting wildly about for something to say to change the subject when someone else did it for her. Lila came into the room, looking around for something. She had changed from her antique traveling suit into a brown tweed skirt, hand-knitted sweater, and Old Maine Trotters that had probably been her mother's shoes. Her Grace Kelly hair was still up in a roll. "Has anyone seen my red notebook?" she asked. "I set it on that table in the front hall with my bag when I came in—"

She'd broken the Dead Ted mood and everybody was grateful. "What did it look like?" Pooky asked.

"About so—" Lila said, indicating a 5 by 7 size with her hands. "It has a bright red cover. It's very important that I find it."

"Like this?" Crispy said, fishing a like object out of her purse.

"Yes, that's it. I should have known you'd take it," Lila said.

If the others were shocked at this rudeness, Crispy seemed delighted. "But I didn't take it. This is mine."

Lila strode across the room and snatched it from Crispy's hand. Crispy grinned as Lila opened the notebook and looked perplexed. "But—this isn't mine," she said.

Crispy took it back with a victorious smile. "I believe I told you that, didn't I?"

"So sorry," Lila said curtly. "I must find mine. I have some very important business numbers in it. Would you all check your things to see if you accidentally picked it up?"

While she was trying, with limited success, to get them to go to their rooms and rummage through their belongings, Jane took the snack tray to the kitchen to refill it. Gordon, the co-owner of the bed and breakfast, had just come in the back door. Edgar introduced him to Jane. Jane gushed about his magnificent decorating while studying him. He was as gorgeous as his creations. He was fortyish, with a thick shock of dark blond hair and Peter Lawford eyes along with a marvelous physique. He seemed genuinely pleased with Jane's remarks, but weary.

"Long day at the factory?" Edgar asked, rolling out some pastry dough.

"The longest. Management's decided to start a new card line with kitten photos. *Kitten photos!* Little kitty turds all over the studio. Cats don't much like having their pictures taken. Just think, if I hadn't taken this job, I'd have never known that. And then I have to come home to this . . . beast!" he said, pointing an accusatory finger at Hector, who yawned magnificently.

"It won't be for long," Edgar assured him. "And Hector caught a chipmunk today. Or at least he found a dead one. It's a step in the right direction. Blood lust is next."

"Excuse me, Jane. I've got to go shower off Eau de Chat," Gordon said. He lightly punched Edgar's shoulder as he passed him and Edgar smiled sympathetically.

"Poor Gordon," Jane said. "He doesn't like Hector?"

"He adores him, but won't admit it," Edgar said.

Mimi Soong pushed the door from the dining room open. "Jane, can I help with anything? Oh, what a wonderful kitchen!"

Edgar wiped the flour off his hands and gave her a tour. They were joined by Pooky a few minutes later—another refugee from Lila's determination to form a search party to hunt for her notebook. Pooky tried to be polite, but it was obvious that a kitchen was a kitchen as far as she was concerned and she wasn't bright enough to pretend real enthusiasm. Mimi, however, knew kitchens and, like an Oriental queen, drifted around asking exactly the right questions. Edgar was delighted.

Jane finally remembered her original errand and put another layer of tiny, crustless sandwiches on the tray, artfully scattered a few olives and carrot curls among them, and took the tray back to the big living room. It was nearly empty. Crispy was fiddling with the television, trying to find the shopping channel, and Kathy was inflicting some tirade on Shelley. Kathy's broad, enthusiastic gestures set her breasts jiggling and swaying in her T-shirt in a way that Jane found both fascinating and horrifying.

". . . and if we then use our right to vote in a way that satisfies our deeper conscience *and* sends a message to the politicians that—"

"Excuse me, Shelley, Edgar wants to know something about your dinner plans," Jane interrupted brutally.

Shelley leaped to her feet like a jack-in-the-box. "Of course!"

"Where are the johns around here?" Kathy asked.

"There's a bathroom with each bedroom," Jane said.

"Oh, all right! We'll finish this discussion later, Shelley," she threatened, heading off toward the stairs.

Shelley sank back into her chair. "That was a lie, wasn't it? About Edgar wanting to talk to me?"

"Sure. So, how's it going?" Jane asked quietly.

"No firearms have been discharged—yet. That's about the best you can say for it. I must be getting credit in heaven for this, mustn't I?"

"I wouldn't count on it," Crispy said from across the room. She had miraculous hearing. She flipped off the television and came to sit with them. "Sorry I didn't rescue you myself," she told Shelley. "And I'm sorry about Kathy. I was really looking forward to seeing her. All that social consciousness was endearing in high school, but so tiresome now."

As she sat down, carefully adjusting her short skirt and silk-clad legs, Avalon drifted into the room carrying a small leather purse with a long, woven strap. She held it awkwardly, as if it weren't hers.

"What's the matter, Avalon?" Crispy asked.

"It's my purse. It's all full of someone else's stuff."

"Whose?"

"I don't know."

She extended the bag to Crispy, who wasn't shy about snooping. She pulled out a billfold and flipped it open. "Pooky," she said. "God, if my driver's license looked like that, I'd give up driving for good. Poor old Pooky."

Jane went to the kitchen door. Beth had joined the kitchen crowd, Mimi had disappeared, and Pooky was standing at the butcher block workstation flipping through a magazine. "Pooky, where's your purse?" Jane asked her.

"Upstairs, I think."

"Would you mind getting it?"

In a few minutes Pooky came in looking spooked. "It's full of your things. Knitting stuff," she said to Avalon. "How did that happen? Where are *my* things?"

Crispy upended Avalon's purse on the coffee table. Beads, fabric scraps, little wads of yarns, and tiny scissors fell out. "Recognize anything?"

They sorted out their belongings while Jane and Shelley exchanged puzzled, and slightly alarmed looks. "One of your Ewe Lambs is a practical joker," Jane said quietly.

"I don't like this, Jane."

"What's not to like?" Jane said. "You're in a house full of women on the brink of menopause, some of whom appear to have come here for the single purpose of tormenting each other, and there's a wolf in sheep's clothing in the bunch."

"Will you stop the puns?"

"I'll try, but they're pretty hard to avoid."

As Jane was helping Edgar clear the table after dinner, he called for everybody's attention. "Ladies, I'll be locking the house up like Fort Knox on the dot of ten-thirty. If you're going out after that, let me know now, and I'll give you a key. Otherwise, you'll have to wake up the whole house to get back in. And I'm a pretty cranky housemother if I have to come down all those stairs after I've gone to bed."

"How peculiar," Lila mused out loud. "To secure a house that doesn't even have locks on the bedroom doors."

Edgar drew himself up, offended. "We were not due to open until next month. The locksmith couldn't get here in time for your visit."

"What difference does it make?" Crispy demanded of Lila. "We were originally supposed to stay at

Shelley's house and she probably doesn't have locks on the bedroom doors either."

"Is anybody going out?" Kathy asked. She'd actually put on a bra under a shapeless tent of a dress for dinner. Her idea of dressing up, Jane supposed.

They glanced around at each other, nobody admitting to having any plans to go out.

Jane, picking up dessert plates, smiled to herself. She was the only one who would have the privilege of leaving tonight.

Or so she thought.

## 6

Shelley hit Jane with the bad news just before eight o'clock. "I have yet *another* favor to ask."

"Hit me," Jane invited.

"Somehow Paul's mother managed to track him down in Singapore—God knows how she does it!— and told him she was having chest pains. As if he could do anything about it from there."

"Oh, no. Is she all right?"

"Of course she's all right. They took her to the emergency room, she threw up some sardines or whatever ghastly thing she'd eaten, and they sent her home. But Paul's frantic. His sister Constanza is staying at my house and just called to say he's calling me back at three in the morning to see how she is."

"Can't Constanza just tell him she's okay?"

"Yes, and I'm sure she has. But Constanza is well-known in the family as the kind of overbearing busy-body who keeps things from people for what she considers Their Own Good. I know he's calling back because he doesn't know whether to believe her or not. I have to be at home when he calls, Jane, and I promised Edgar I'd stay here tonight to keep an eye on the Ewe Lambs."

"Why? They're grown women."

"But I'm the hostess. I think Edgar has horrific

visions of somebody wanting a tampon in the middle of the night or something."

"So you need me to stay in your place?"

"Would you? Could you? I'll take your kids to my house . . . for the next couple of *years* if you'd like."

"No, they can stay alone. Mike's there and responsible. But I'll have to go home first and put out any family forest fires that have broken out during the evening."

Edgar insisted on walking Jane to her car and seeing that she was safely locked in before she left. She rolled the window down an inch and said, "Dinner was wonderful, Edgar. I'll be back in twenty or thirty minutes. You'll survive this visitation."

He laughed. "I know I will. I once catered a convention of farm equipment salesmen. After that, life's easy."

Jane went home and was astonished to discover that the kids had cleaned up the kitchen after dinner. Her sixth grade son Todd had even gone to bed without being told. A worrisome thing. She went into his room, scuffling her feet gingerly to avoid stepping on Legos in her bare feet, and felt his forehead. No fever.

Katie was on the upstairs hall phone, which was strictly forbidden after ten, and quickly hung up when Jane glared at her. She flounced off to her room. Jane followed her and inquired if there had been any messages for her during the evening, even though she knew it would have been impossible for Mel to get through Katie's talkfest. Out of self-defense, Jane was going to have to get Katie her own phone line. She explained to Katie that she was going back to the bed and breakfast, but would return early to help get everybody off to school.

Jane's son Mike was sitting in a nest of paperwork on the living room sofa with MTV blaring in the background. Jane turned the sound down. "What's all this, college stuff again?"

"Geez, Mom, if you knew enough to fill in all these application forms and scholarship requests, you wouldn't need to go to college. How about I just go to plumbing school?"

"College first. Then plumbing school for postgraduate work."

"What am I going to do about letters of recommendation?"

"What do you mean? You've got several good ones. Your band teacher, the manager of the grocery store where you worked last summer, your uncle—"

"Yeah, but they aren't anybody important. Scott's got one from *his* uncle who's a state senator. My uncle's just a pharmacist. Don't we know anybody important? Maybe Grumps knows some big deal in the State Department?"

"Your grandfather knows everybody in the State Department, but they don't know *you*."

"So? All I need is their stationery," he said with a grin.

Jane laughed. "You'll do fine with what you've got, honey. With your test scores and your grades, any college would be nuts to pass you up."

"Aw, that's Mom Talk."

"That's what I'm for," Jane said. She explained the revised plan for the night. "You better get to bed."

Jane helped him get his papers straightened up, then let Willard the Cowardly Dog out one more time before she went up the steps with Willard panting at her heels and Max and Meow weaving around her feet. The cats loved it when Jane went up to bed, apparently because it meant the next thing she'd do would be to get up in the morning and feed them. Willard always slept with Todd, but the cats slept in Jane's room so they were on hand when she woke up. "Sorry, guys, but I'm not staying," she told them.

Jane dumped her clothes in the dry-cleaning heap in her closet, and put on jeans and a sweatshirt. Leaving the cats watching her in perplexity, she grabbed a few necessities, locked up the house, and went back to the bed and breakfast.

"I've put you in the Cary Grant room," Edgar said when she got out of the car. He'd been waiting for her at the back door. "It's Hector's favorite place. And I've told the others where to find you if they need anything."

Jane went upstairs and made herself comfortable in the room she was assigned. Hector did follow her, but didn't seem ready to settle down for the night any more than the Ewe Lambs did. Jane could hear them down the hall laughing and talking. She got into bed, turned out the lights, and smiled to herself. The house wasn't terribly well soundproofed and she could still hear them a little. Except that the voices were a little bit lower, a bit more restrained, it sounded just like her house did when Katie had friends for a sleepover.

She had to be up early and tried to will herself to fall straight to sleep, but it was impossible. Not because of the voices, but because her mind kept replaying snippets of the evening.

Some parts of it had been fun. Crispy had told some really funny stories about her various moneyed marriages. But between stories on herself, she managed to slip in quite a few uncomfortable ones about the others. "Remember that time you went around with the toilet paper stuck to your shoe all day, Pooky, and nobody told you?" she said as if it were hilarious. She also managed to remind Kathy of the time she'd planned the giant protest rally and it rained and nobody showed up except the newspaper reporters she'd invited.

Lila was even worse. Where Crispy's taunts and digs were fairly harmless and most were delivered with apparent affectionate memory, Lila's were vaguely ominous. She reminisced at some length about a slumber party, the point of the story seeming to be that Avalon was into drug use then and probably still was. She suggested, without actually saying so, that this might have accounted for the switch in purse contents—that "somebody" expected to find suspicious substances in either Pooky's purse or Avalon's.

Later on Lila made a point of bringing up the gossip about Beth's possible Supreme Court appointment. "Think of the scrutiny, Beth," she said. "Every aspect of your life under a public microscope. We'll all watch the hearings and I bet we learn things about you we never knew."

But Beth wasn't playing. "I doubt it," she said with a bored smile. "I'm not that interesting."

"None of us are," Kathy said with a laugh.

"Oh, I don't know. I'll bet anybody who turned a spotlight on you would learn some fascinating things," Lila said to her.

Kathy blushed and blustered and left the room.

When Lila turned her malevolent attention to Mimi, she failed utterly. "Soong . . ." she said as if talking to herself. "Rather a famous Chinese name for an American to have."

"Isn't it?" Mimi answered. To the questioning looks of the others, she said, "There were three Soong sisters in China. One married Sun Yat-sen, one married

Chiang Kai-shek and the other . . . I've forgotten what the other one did. No relation to my husband though. It's a very common name."

"I'm surprised that somebody so 'aggressively' American would marry anyone of Chinese descent," Lila went on.

Mimi just laughed and turned to Jane to explain. "Lila, in her subtle way, is referring to the fact that I once wanted to be Doris Day and Sandra Dee all in one. I wish you could have seen me—oh, I forgot! I brought yearbooks."

She had dashed off to get them while Jane wandered into the kitchen where Edgar and Gordon were playing gin rummy at the table. Kathy was there, too, leaning into the gigantic open refrigerator, her oversized derriere sticking out obstructing traffic. "Has anybody killed her yet?" she asked as Jane edged around her.

"Who? Lila? Not yet."

Pooky had followed Jane through the door. "Then I'll volunteer." She squeezed around Jane and Kathy and headed for the back door. "She just got through reminding everybody in the living room that I'm a year older than the rest of you because I was held back that year I had mono and missed so much school!"

"Poor thing. Sick *and* stupid," Kathy muttered into the refrigerator.

Fortunately Pooky didn't hear this. She asked Edgar, "May I go outside? I just want some fresh air."

"Sure," Edgar replied, laying out his cards smugly. "I won't lock up for another hour yet."

"I only want to go out for a few minutes. I always take a walk before going to bed. It helps me sleep," Pooky said, making a hair-tossing gesture which failed because her stiff, thin hair had no "toss" left in it.

\*     \*     \*

Max interrupted Jane's thoughts by walking across
her seeking a warm corner to curl into. It took her a
second to realize it wasn't her own Max, it was Hector. She sat up and gave him a chin chuck. He settled
into the crook of her knees. Jane adjusted to make
room for him. If only she could fall asleep like he
could. Maybe it had to do with being able to purr. . . .

Her last thoughts were of the school yearbook Mimi
brought out. Mimi's senior photo was hysterical. She
actually had a platinum blond flip hairdo and raccoon
makeup designed to disguise her Oriental eyes. Which
it didn't. "Pooky did my hair. It took so much bleach
her fingers peeled for a week," Mimi said, giggling.
"I don't know why my mother didn't just drown me
and spare herself the misery of having me around."

Jane fell asleep smiling.


At first she dreamed she heard the light tapping, then
gradually awoke to realize it was somebody at her door.
She stumbled over and opened it. Beth Vaughn was
standing in the hallway wearing a sensible tailored
robe. "Jane, I'm awfully sorry to wake you up," she
whispered. "But I have a problem. Can you hear it?"

Jane stepped into the hallway. A faint ding-ding-
ding was sounding someplace. "What's that?" she
asked stupidly.

"I don't know. I think it's a smoke alarm, but
there's no smoke and it's not loud enough. I can't
find it."

As they padded toward Beth's room, Avalon's door
opened. Her red hair was in wild disarray. "What's
that bell?" she asked.

"We don't know," Jane replied. "We're trying to
find it."

By the time they located the source of the sound, half the Ewe Lambs were up and roaming the hallway. It turned out to be a cheap alarm clock stuck into the glass bowl of the overhead light fixture in Beth's bedroom. Beth, a little taller than the rest, climbed a chair and retrieved it. "Who in the world would have put it there and set it to go off?" she asked.

"Pretty damned inconsiderate trick if you ask me," Kathy groused. "I'm going back to bed."

Nobody was in much of a mood to discuss the alarm clock. "Let's all go back to bed," Jane said, taking the alarm clock from Beth.

Jane found it hard to get back to sleep. She had nearly dropped off when someone sat down on her bed.

She bolted upright, barely containing a scream.

But it was only Hector. "Geez, Hector, you scared the stuffing out of me," she said, petting him. Then she realized that the last time she'd seen him he was in the hallway getting underfoot. She was sure she'd shut him out of her room when she went back to bed, but here he was. Maybe he'd pushed the door open. But no, she could see in the dim, reflected glow of the moon that her door was tightly closed. *How did he get in here?*

It was a mild night and the window was open, but she was on the second floor. Curious, she got up and looked out. Yes, there were sturdy vines outside. Hector could have climbed them. But that presupposed he was starting from outdoors and she knew he had been indoors. Still, he might have some other means of leaving the house. It was a big, old place and might well have some other cat-sized escape routes. Still, it was strange and a little alarming.

And in that frame of mind, she settled back into

bed and could hear a thousand suspicious sounds. The creaking in the hallway sounded like a furtive tread on the old stairs, the clattering of leaves outside the window being stirred by a breeze sounded like little creatures scrabbling around. Little red-eyed creatures, she thought and shuddered. She had just managed to clear this scary thought from her mind when she heard another ding-ding-ding. By the time she got to her door this time, Mimi was standing outside it, hand raised to knock. Mimi still looked cool and serene and her hair wasn't even mussed, but she was cranky. "I'm sorry," she said curtly. "Would you help me find the damned thing before it wakes everybody again?"

This time the clock was in Mimi's bathroom cabinet.

And the one that went off at four o'clock was between the mattresses in Kathy's room.

The next alarm clock that went off was Jane's own that she'd brought from home. She fumbled for it, turned it off, then looked blearily around the room, for the moment not remembering where she was. She got dressed quietly and quickly, and crept downstairs to let herself out. It was just seven when she got home.

When she got back to the bed and breakfast an hour and a half later, the back door to the kitchen stood open. "Edgar? I'm sorry I'm late. Katie lost her lunch ticket and missed her car pool—"

Edgar was sitting at the kitchen table reading the paper. "No hurry. We had a long night here as you well know."

Jane poured herself a cup of his miracle coffee and sat down. "So you heard the commotion."

"I stayed out of it, but couldn't help but hear the noise and eavesdrop."

"Edgar, I don't get it. I just don't have the mind-set for practical jokes. I can't think them up. I don't think they're funny. At least these seem harmless. Nobody can get hurt when an alarm goes off. That's not like exploding cigars or something. So everybody's sleeping in?"

"Not everybody. Shelley's in the living room. She got here about ten minutes ago. And somebody else went through here and had coffee while I was back upstairs. Left a coffee cup in the sink."

Gordon stumbled into the room in jeans and a sweatshirt, his hair rumpled and sheet-creases on his cheek. "My God, what was that? An old-fashioned slumber party? Or did I imagine noises all night?"

Edgar explained. "Crazy," Gordon mumbled, pouring himself a gigantic mug of coffee.

"You're not working today?" Jane asked him when he finally raised his face from the mug.

"Not at the salt mines. I told Edgar I'd hang around in case he needed me."

"The only assistance I need now is getting breakfast into these women. It would help if they got up. Jane, you want to see if you can stir them?"

Jane obediently went up the front stairs. Before she even reached the second floor, she could hear somebody tapping on a door and saying something. But there wasn't anybody in the hallway. She went along and discovered that the sound was coming from the apricot room, which was assigned to Avalon.

"Avalon?" she said to the closed door.

"Thank God! Get me out of here. The doorknob came off in my hand."

Jane looked down and sure enough, there was just a hole where the post of the old-fashioned doorknob should have been. Someone had removed the outer knob so that the inner knob simply pulled out when Avalon tried to open the door. Jane fetched Edgar, who instructed her to reinsert the post so he could turn it with pliers from the outside. But by the time this was completed, they discovered that Pooky's and Beth's doors had also been rigged and they had to be rescued.

It was a cranky flock of Ewe Lambs that finally started drifting down to the aroma of coffee and bacon. "This is a nightmare, Jane," Shelley said from where she hunched in the living room pretending to watch the morning news. "Edgar told me about last night and the clocks. I'm sorry you were stuck with that."

"It's okay. It wasn't your fault. Did Paul call?"

"He did. And was reassured, but I couldn't get back to sleep. And there are still days of this ahead before it's over!"

"Yes, but look at it this way: one whole day of it is behind you. And I found all the missing doorknobs in the flour canister. So that problem's taken care of."

"I hate chirpy people," Shelley said.

"Oh? I thought you'd prefer chirping to baa-ing," Jane said, making a dreadful sheep noise. She went back to the kitchen smiling. This was a rare treat, seeing Shelley at her wit's end. Shelley never lost control of herself or a situation and here she was more tired and rattled than Jane herself.

Jane helped Edgar fix English muffins that were toasted with a rich cheddar cheese topping, shirred eggs with mushrooms and minced basil from a pot on the windowsill, and an arrangement of kiwi and strawberry slices. At least, she tried to help him. Mainly she got in his way, oohing and aahing and taking mental note of the ingredients.

By the time the breakfast was ready, Shelley had gotten a grip on herself. "Ladies, we need to get breakfast over and begin our meeting," she was saying as she shooed them toward the dining room. "We really have a lot of business to work out if we're going to contribute to the fund-raising effort."

Jane took in the tray of fruit and said, "Who's missing?"

They all glanced around at each other. "Where's Lila?" Beth asked. "She's not locked in her room, too, is she?"

Shelley went up to see and came down perplexed. "She's not there. It doesn't look like her bed's been slept in."

"Or maybe she made it herself," Jane said, hoping some of the others would follow this example and save her some maid duties.

"Maybe she went out running," Crispy said. "Didn't she mention—jogging?" She shuddered as she said the word.

"Well, if she did, she better be back by the time we start the meeting," Shelley said firmly. Crispy and Avalon looked at her with surprise. Just as Jane had never seen Shelley out of control, these women must not have seen her *in* control.

But Lila hadn't turned up by nine-thirty when the meeting was supposed to start. Shelley went back upstairs when it was proposed that Lila might have actually left and gone home. But her belongings were still there. They all seemed to feel they ought to be concerned about Lila, but were relieved to have her out of their hair.

Shelley marched them all to the library while Jane collected her cleaning supplies and went upstairs. The first room she tackled was Avalon's, which was surprisingly neat considering Avalon's untidy appearance. When she got to the bathroom, she realized she'd forgotten to bring along toilet paper and the roll in Avalon's bathroom needed replacing.

Jane went back downstairs to the supply closet, discovered there was only one roll left there and headed out to the carriage house where the huge carton was stored. She pulled open the small door set into the big garage door and stepped into the gloom. Edgar had turned on a light when they were here before. Where was the switch? She fumbled along the adjacent wall for a moment before she found it.

When the light came on, she noticed two things right away that shouldn't have been there. Against the far wall there was a six-pack of beer with two cans opened and cigarettes scattered next to it. But her attention to this was short-lived when she noticed the pile of curtains and draperies that were being turned into cleaning rags.

There was a woman's hand protruding from them.

Her heart pounding in her throat, Jane stood rooted for a second, unable to breathe or even think. Then, leaden-footed, she went forward and gingerly removed some of the rags.

It was, as she expected, Lila. And she was very dead.

## 7

Jane hadn't anticipated seeing Mel VanDyne until the following Tuesday, but his was the face she saw when she removed the cold compress from her eyes. She was sitting in Edgar's kitchen, where she had very nearly fainted after telling him what was in the carriage house. Edgar had pushed her into a chair, shoved her head between her knees, and gone to look for himself, reappearing seconds later to dial the police. Then, while they waited the few minutes it took the law to arrive, he'd made her an ice pack and insisted that she slouch back in the chair and apply it to her eyes. "My mother believed in this as a cure for any shock," he said, his own voice trembling a little. "Hold still!"

In quick succession, three sirens wailed to a stop in the drive, half a dozen car doors slammed. Edgar went out the kitchen door to show the police to the scene. Shelley's control over her meeting had apparently evaporated, because within moments, the kitchen was full of women asking what was happening. Jane stayed hidden behind her cold compress, thinking like mad.

Finally Shelley said to her, "Jane, what's this about?"

"Lila's out there. Dead," Jane mumbled.

A shocked silence.

The kitchen door opened and Mel said, "Jane . . . Mrs. Jeffry?"

*Uh-oh,* Jane thought. *He's calling me Mrs. Jeffry. Not a good sign.* She removed the compress. "Yes?"

"I understand you found the body?"

"I'm afraid so."

"Is there someplace we can speak privately?"

"Use the library," Shelley said.

"Ah, Mrs. Nowack, you're here too," Mel said blandly.

"As a matter of fact, I am, Detective VanDyne."

They were always nasty-polite to each other. Jane had first met Mel when Shelley's cleaning lady had met a bad end in Shelley's guest room. They had "taken exception" to each other, to put it mildly, then and didn't seem to be able to get over it. Jane led the way to the library amid a hum of speculation from the Ewe Lambs, and closed the door.

Mel closed the door and then grabbed Jane by the shoulders. He looked as if he was debating between shaking her hard and hugging her. Finally he just released her, sighed, and sat down in one of the leather sofas. "So, Jane, what the hell are you doing finding bodies?" he said with forced calm.

"It's not as if I meant to, Mel. I'd have been thrilled if somebody else had found her."

"And so would I! I hate that you were here at all where somebody's been killed. Try to be very precise and tell me what's going on here," he said, taking out a notebook and clicking a nice gold pen. Jane found herself thinking it looked like the kind of pen people only had as gifts and wondered who gave it to him.

"Okay, Shelley went to a high school here that had a big fire and since the high school reunion is taking place this weekend, she invited some of the women in a do-gooder club they had in school to come early and plan fund-raising."

He wrote for a moment and glanced up at her, smiling. "That *was* concise! Now, what have you got to do with it?"

Jane explained how she'd been roped into helping Edgar and being Shelley's "date." This wasn't quite as concise, but she managed it fairly well.

"Who's the one in the carriage house? What do you know about her?" Mel asked.

"She's just one of them. A nasty one, actually. She was being very unpleasant yesterday."

"Is that when they all came?"

"Yes, at various times during the day."

"When did you last see her? The victim?"

"You say 'victim' as in murder? She didn't die of natural causes, then?"

He didn't even respond to this except to cock his eyebrow.

"I see," Jane said. "Let me think . . . I don't know exactly when I last saw her. She was at dinner. She was making nasty cracks to people off and on all evening. But everybody was milling around. Going upstairs for things, talking in the library and the living room. Coming in and out of the kitchen. I was mostly in the kitchen and only saw the people who came through there."

"Try to pin down the last time you're sure you saw her," Mel insisted, not sympathetic to Jane's excuses.

"Okay. Dinner for sure. That was at seven. I came in the kitchen just after Lila had been trying to goad Mimi Soong about something. That's the last time I actually saw her."

"When was that?"

"I have no idea. I wasn't paying any attention to the time. Oh, wait. Pooky came in a little bit after that and Lila had been harassing her and Pooky said she wanted to go outside for some air and Edgar said he wasn't going to lock up for an hour yet, so it must have been about nine-thirty because he locked up at ten-thirty, just after I got back."

Mel had been staring at her intently. "Pooky?" he said, pronouncing it very carefully. "That's somebody's name?"

"A nickname, I think. A couple of them go by nicknames. Lila was actually Delilah, I think."

"All right, give me a rundown on who's attending this thing, who was in the house last night."

"Me, for one."

"What about Mrs. Nowack?"

"She had to go home to wait for a phone call from her husband. And of course, Edgar and Gordon were here. It's their house."

"The guests . . . ?" he prodded.

"All right, there was Lila. I can't remember her last name, though. And Beth . . . uh, Vaughn, I think. She's the one who's a judge. Very square, sensible, low-heeled shoes, graying hair."

VanDyne closed his eyes for a second, then nodded, as if he'd seen her in the kitchen and identified her.

"And Crispy. I'm sorry I'm rattled. I can't remember her real name either. Her maiden name was Crisp. She's the little stylish one with the spike heels, frosted hair, and incredible fingernails. Avalon Smith is the one with the sloppy dark red hair and potato sack clothing. She's from Arkansas."

"Who else?"

"Pooky is that poor woman with the horrible face-lift that went wrong and the stiff blond hair that looks like a bad wig. She seems to be stunningly stupid, so keep that in mind when you talk to her."

"I'll do that," he said wryly. "Who's the fat, sloppy one in the carpenter overalls?"

"Kathy Herrmannson. She sees herself as the social conscience of the group. Peace, love, and recycling."

"Is that all?"

"I think s—no, I left out Mimi Soong. She's Chinese and very elegant."

Mel sat back for a moment, digesting this information. Finally he said, "Got any idea who did it?"

"Killed her? No. I think everybody would have liked to. There were jokes about drawing straws."

"Who made the jokes?"

"I won't answer that!" Jane said. "They were just jokes, because she was so unpleasant. I don't even remember who said what. Somebody was also playing practical jokes."

"Oh? What kind? Who'd they play them on?"

"Somebody exchanged the contents of Avalon's and Pooky's purses."

"So?"

"So, nothing. It was dumb and pointless. Then alarm clocks went off all night. Cheap wind-up ones somebody had hidden in a couple of rooms. And this morning, some of the doorknobs had been taken off the outsides of bedroom doors so people couldn't get out until Edgar rescued them. None of the tricks were particularly clever or even funny, just stupid nuisances."

Mel sat back and tented his fingers. "Odd," he murmured.

"Mel—was it my imagination, or were there beer cans and cigarettes on the floor out there in the carriage house?"

"There were."

"They weren't supposed to be there."

"No, probably not."

"Then you don't suspect any of the Ewe Lambs."

"The *what?*"

"Ewe Lambs. That's what the club was called."

"Grown women—"

"They weren't grown women when they joined, Mel. It's an old club, named before political correctness was the in thing. Back to the beer and cigarettes—"

"The cans are being fingerprinted."

"So you do think it was an outsider."

"Probably so. This place had quite a reputation in the drug trade until recently."

There was a knock on the door and before Mel could speak, Edgar rushed in. "Detective VanDyne? You're in charge here?" He introduced himself quickly, then said, "Look here, you've got to get to the bottom of this and get the killer out of my house!"

"Edgar!" Jane exclaimed. "It wasn't one of the Ewe Lambs, it was somebody from outside."

Edgar glared at her and VanDyne held his hands up for silence. "Hold it! We don't have any idea yet how it happened and we *will* thoroughly investigate all possibilities."

"Mel! You just said—" Jane began.

But he cut her off. "My personal opinion and my professional duties are not the same thing, Jane. Now, if you'll get your things, I'll have an officer drive you home."

"Home? Why?"

He looked at her as if she'd lost her mind. "Because there's been a murder here, that's why."

"So you're making everybody leave?" Jane asked, wanting to make quite certain she understood before she took a policy position.

"No, not everybody. And I'm not 'making' you

leave. Just offering you the opportunity—which any sensible person would take, I might add."

"Sensible," Jane said very softly, her eyes narrowing. "I may not be sensible, Detective VanDyne, but I am loyal to my friends and keep up my part of bargains. I told Edgar I'd skivvy and skivvy I will!"

Edgar's expression softened as Mel's took on a cold, professional look. "Fine. Do as you like. But as your friend, your *good* friend, I'd advise you to go home."

That made her feel a tad guilty. "Sorry, Mel. I do have to stay with Shelley and Edgar."

Mel wasn't placated. "Mr. North, may I use this room to question people? Starting with you?"

As Jane left, Mel opened the door for her and touched her shoulder lightly as she passed through. It was a tiny thing, but amazingly intimate, considering the situation.

She found most of the rest of the women, plus Gordon, who was fixing a lamp cord in the corner, in the living room. Kathy jumped up. "Jane, for God's sakes, you shouldn't let the pigs question you without your attorney!"

"Pigs?" Jane said. "That 'pig' is a fine, honorable man!" Thank God he didn't hear her coming to his defense. "Anyway, he wasn't questioning me. Not exactly. Not like a suspect or anything. Nobody's a suspect. It's just his job to find out what happened to Lila and I assume everybody's interested in knowing that."

"Jane's quite right," Beth said calmly without looking up from the file folder in her lap. "They're following a well-established and absolutely necessary routine. I saw them taking beer cans out in plastic bags for fingerprinting and DNA analysis of any residual saliva. They're doing a cautious, thorough investigation and none of us need worry. We were all locked in here overnight." She pulled out a paper, frowned, and put it back into the folder.

"Yeah, well you'd have to say that, Ms. Law and Order," Kathy said.

"Kathy, I'm a judge," Beth said with a remarkably tolerant smile. "I'm supposed to be in favor of law and order. Are you admitting you'd prefer anarchy, with somebody railroaded into jail? Or just taken out and hanged?"

"Of course not!"

"Then pay attention. I've been on the bench for several murder cases and believe me, the police must collect every scrap of evidence and information that they can before they can even begin to speculate on the reasons and method. They're doing their job and I suggest we all cooperate with them. It's the only sensible thing. There's obviously a dangerous criminal out there who must be apprehended."

"Out there—or in here," Crispy said from the corner of the room.

An electrified silence fell. Crispy looked around at them all, then pushed the television control button. A shampoo commercial blared at them.

Mimi was standing next to Jane. "That's the one thing I don't think anybody really needed to say," she whispered.

# — 8 —

Shelley followed Jane to the kitchen. Gordon was at the far end, grimly watching police activity in the back parking lot. "What are they doing?" Jane asked.

"Not much now," Gordon said, coming away from the window. "They've taken away the body. And bags and bags of stuff. Now they're measuring things."

"Why's Edgar determined to pin this on the Ewe Lambs?" Jane asked bluntly.

"Is he?" Gordon asked. "Makes sense. It wouldn't do us any good if it were known that this was a dangerous place to stay. But if one of the women staying here did it, why that's no reflection on us at all."

"I hadn't thought of that," Jane said. "When did she go out there? How did she do it? I know Edgar locks up carefully."

"Yes, but he didn't take roll call, you know. If that had been necessary, it would have been *your* job," Gordon said a little impatiently. "She either went out there before he locked up, or she let herself out afterwards. The doors work that way; they have to in case of fire. You can go out when they're locked, but they're all balanced to swing shut and relock. The bedroom doors will be like that, too, when they're done."

"When did you last see her?" Jane asked Gordon.

"Me? I don't know. I don't even know which one got killed. I wasn't paying attention."

"She went up to her room about nine-thirty," Shelley said. "At least, I assume that's where she went. She left the living room then."

"She didn't go out the kitchen door between then and ten because I was there the whole time," Jane said. "Except when I went into the library to look for my purse . . ." She trailed off.

"The police have their work cut out for them if they're trying to put together a timetable of what went on inside the house," Shelley said. "How many other outside doors are there, Gordon?"

"Dozens," he said grimly. "The front door, the French doors from the living room. A door on the third floor leading down an outside stairway. A door at the end of the utility room. Then there's a door from the deck—"

"Never mind. I get the picture," Shelley said.

"Is Edgar still with the detective?" Gordon asked. "I think I'll just see what's going on."

When he'd left the room, Shelley said, "What do you suppose really happened, Jane?"

"I don't know. There were beer cans on the floor out there and a spilled pack of cigarettes. I would guess she interrupted some tramps or drug dealers or something who were out there and they killed her."

"But what was she doing out there?"

Jane shrugged. "Just snooping around? Who knows? She did seem to have an obscene interest in everybody else's business. And the building is where Ted died. I notice everyone made a point of not mentioning that last night. Except when Avalon brought out that picture. I wonder if Pooky managed to get it away from her. Poor Avalon. Anyway, maybe it was just ghoulish curiosity about the place on Lila's part."

"Well, whatever it was, I've got to get my meeting back under way," Shelley said. "And your friend VanDyne is using the library. How long do you think he'll be?"

"Shelley, you'll never get everybody to settle down and talk about fund-raising! There's been a murder on the doorstep!"

Shelley considered this. "Maybe I *should* wait until afternoon."

"That makes me think; I've got jobs to do, too. I was looking for loo paper when I found her. I'm going back to work."

Jane went back upstairs, passing Pooky coming down. Ewe Lambs were spread out all over the house, some talking quietly, others doing paperwork or flipping through magazines. Jane went back to Avalon's room and found that there was a vast stash of toilet paper in the cabinet under the sink. She finished up the apricot room and went on to Kathy's, which was—not surprisingly—a mess. Clothes were strewn everywhere, a damp washcloth was on the floor making a spot on the carpet. An ashtray had spilled on the floor. And she'd have to do the bed from scratch. She tossed Kathy's cheesy plastic purse on the overstuffed chair by the window and started to work.

She kept thinking back to her conversation with Mel. And she found herself wondering what on earth Lila was really doing out in the carriage house. With her Grace Kelly hair and antique clothing and cool, nasty manner, Lila didn't seem the type to be a thrill-seeker who'd visit the scene of Ted Francisco's suicide. And she didn't seem to have any particular interest in Ted's death. Of course, they had all avoided mentioning him, so maybe that wasn't a fair assessment.

Still, what *had* she been doing in the carriage house? And when had she gone out there? She'd been present at dinner when Edgar made his strong warning about locking up at ten-thirty. If she went out before that, she probably assumed she'd be back in before the deadline. Then, too, she might well have been arrogant enough that it didn't matter. She didn't seem the type to care much if she disturbed someone else's rest. But if she went out later—why?

She had, of course, grown up in the neighborhood. Or at least lived here during high school. Maybe she still had acquaintances here and was going out to meet somebody. Somebody she shouldn't have met, obviously.

When Jane finished with the bed, she realized that Kathy's purse had slid off the chair and dumped its contents all over the floor. She started to put things back when she realized just what those contents were.

A slim-banded gold watch with diamonds around the face; a ring that featured an enormous dark pink stone that had to be a ruby. Stunned and curious, Jane opened the lizard-skin billfold and found a Gold Visa card, a Gold American Express card, and a checkbook showing a balance of $23,683.

"What have you got there?" Crispy said from the doorway. She came in and gently closed the door behind her.

"She's rich," Jane said, too astonished at the discovery to be embarrassed at being caught snooping.

"Of course she is. Couldn't you tell?"

"No! How could anybody tell?"

"Easy, my dear. If you know what to look for," Crispy said, taking the billfold from Jane and flipping through it before she put it back in the ratty plastic purse. "The hands always give it away. You just need a quick glance at those cuticles to realize they've had at least ten years of manicures. And the slight tan line where she normally wears a watch and ring. Why would a person who always wears those take them off unless they conflicted with the image she's trying to project?"

"But why? Why pretend to be a poor slob? I'm always trying to pretend I'm *not* a poor slob!" she added with a laugh.

"Just a guess—she didn't want everybody to know she'd sold out to the establishment. She was a fiery liberal, convinced she'd change the world by sheer force of personality and righteousness. It was her claim to fame. Instead, she ends up a capitalist pig."

"So this scratching a living out of the dirt in Oklahoma and picking up cans and bottles at the roadside to save the earth is just made up?" Jane said, still not quite convinced in spite of the evidence.

"The little subsistence farm in Oklahoma is probably a thousand square acres of wall-to-wall oil wells."

"Amazing!"

"Rule One of Reunions, Jane. Nobody is what they seem."

"Including you?"

"No, I'm the exception," Crispy said with a wry grin. "Actually, I came looking for you to ask a favor. The Joker has been at it again and all my underwear is missing."

"You're kidding. This is ridiculous. And stealing underwear is nasty and creepy. Why is somebody doing this stuff?"

"Who knows? Somebody apparently thinks it's funny. Would you drive me to a mall to pick up a few things?"

"Sure, but we'll have to make it fast. I've got to get all the rooms cleaned."

Elegant nails flashing, Crispy waved this away as a minor consideration.

Mel was gone. Jane reported where she was going to Shelley, then asked permission of the police who were still working around the carriage house. After taking their names, the officer in charge let them leave.

They were only halfway to the mall when Crispy said, "Oops, I've lost my earring. Would you mind stopping to let me look for it?"

Crispy didn't even bother to look around the front seat, but stepped out and started searching the back. Jane watched her.

"Maybe you should look in your purse, Crispy," she suggested.

"Purse?" Crispy answered, her voice muffled as she rummaged under the backseat.

"Yes, I saw you put it in there as we started out."

Crispy lifted her head and grinned. "I should have known you'd be too smart to be fooled. I *do* like you."

"What are you really looking for?"

"That notebook."

"Notebook . . . ? Oh, yes. The one Lila was looking for last night." Jane should have mentioned that to Mel. There was probably a lot she should have mentioned to him, come to think of it. She hadn't even told him about Dead Ted.

"Uh-huh, that's the one. She had it out in the car yesterday. I noticed it was just like mine, so I managed to shove it off the seat and replace it with my own."

"So the one she brought inside and put on the hall table was really yours?"

"I just scooped it back up when she wasn't looking."

"But why?"

"Curiosity. I just wanted to see what she kept in it and the opportunity presented itself." She leaned back over and reached farther under the seat. "Ah, here it is."

"We'll go back and give it to the police," Jane said.

"Why on earth would we do that?"

"Because, in case you hadn't noticed, the owner has been murdered!"

"By drug dealers roaming the neighborhood. The notebook has nothing to do with it. And I will give it to them anyway. After I've taken a look at it. Now, lead me to the lingerie!"

She hopped back into the front seat and sat there looking like a happy puppy getting to go for a ride. Jane started the engine. "I'm going to tell the police you have that. . . . *after* you show it to me," she said.

Crispy grinned. "A woman after my own heart— such as it is."

## 9

Jane let Crispy out at the mall and cruised the parking lot. She hoped Crispy had left the notebook in the car so she could take a quick look, but there was no sign of it. Crispy emerged in a remarkably short time with a shopping bag and they drove back to the bed and breakfast. There was still one police car in the back drive, so Jane parked in front. Crispy hopped out of the car, gushing thanks, and Jane followed more slowly. She wished she could stay outside and enjoy the day. September could be a replay of August, hot and oppressive, but today was one of those September beauties that made a person remember how nice autumn could be. The air, while not chilly, was fresh and clean-smelling. Jane could imagine, if not actually smell, woodsmoke and the tang of apple cider.

As Jane reached the front door, she nearly collided with the mailman, whom she hadn't noticed approaching. There was a slot next to the door and he was struggling to force a large, stiff envelope into it. "I'll take it in," she said, taking the wad of mail from him.

She automatically sorted the mail into a pile for Gordon, a pile for Edgar, and an enormous stack for "Occupant," and set the three stacks on the front hall table as she passed through. Mimi came down the stairs wearing a red silk tunic over black trousers and clutching a school yearbook. "I hear you had to take

Crispy shopping," she said. "That must have been a thrill. I bet she goes through a department store like the plague."

"I was spared the sight," Jane said. "I drove around looking for a parking place. She was awfully fast, though. I imagine there are saleswomen still weeping and pressing cologne-drenched hankies to their temples."

Mimi laughed. "This is crazy. Who would steal her underwear and why?"

Jane shrugged, a corner of her mind still picking over the mail.

"Shelley held a gun to our heads while you were gone and made us clean up our rooms like good little girls."

"Did she? Thank goodness. It's already noon and I'd only done two rooms. May I look at the yearbook? Will you show me everybody?"

They went into the living room and Mimi insisted on waiting on Jane for a change. While she was fetching them Cokes, Jane idly flipped through the book. Pooky came in the room, glanced around as if looking for something, and left. Jane could hear shrill laughter upstairs. Some of them must have gathered in one of the bedrooms to gossip. In spite of everything, they were having a good time. At least, most of them were. She caught a glimpse of Beth through the French windows. She was strolling outdoors, hands behind her back, head down, deep in thought. It made a nice picture, the renowned judge in a moment of contemplative leisure against a background of glossy rhododendron bushes and tidy chrysanthemums loaded with fat buds. Hector, the Siamese cat, was strolling along behind her, adding immeasurably to the domesticity of the picture.

Mimi returned with their drinks and a plate of sandwiches and chips. "You missed lunch."

"Lunch! Oh, my God! I was supposed to be helping Edgar."

"It's all right. He just put out sandwich fixings and we helped ourselves. Edgar's idea of sandwich fillings includes pâtés, and anchovy butter. We're not talking processed cheese here," she said.

"Who's Gloria Kevitch?" Jane asked, taking a bite of a deviled ham sandwich on homemade rye bread. Oh, that Edgar!

"Gloria who?"

"Gloria Kevitch. The yearbook is dedicated to her."

Mimi looked puzzled for a second before a light dawned. "Oh, yes. A girl in our class who died. It was supposed to be a car accident, but it was widely assumed to have been suicide."

"Two suicides in one class?"

"Unfortunately, yes."

"Was she a Ewe Lamb?"

"Good heavens, no. She was an ordinary person. Ewe Lambs were all from the 'top drawer.' " She spoke with heavy, unpleasant irony. "Poor Gloria. She was in my gym class and was a cute, funny girl, if a bit hyper. She tried to get into the club, but she was voted down. It's amazing to me to think back to how much it meant to us then. And it was so silly and snobbish. But then, so were we."

Jane just nodded and kept eating, encouraging her to go on.

"My parents came to this country as adults, fleeing the onset of the so-called Cultural Revolution of which Dad would have been one of the first victims. My dad was a math professor, could speak English, and got a good job. Drove a Ford, bought a lawnmower, ate

Twinkies. But my mother was very old-country. She couldn't learn the language, thought Western clothes were ugly and immodest, hid in the house. I was so ashamed of her. Now I realize she must have been desperately ashamed of me. I wanted to be an American Girl. More American than Americans. Well, you saw the picture I showed you yesterday. I was grotesque."

Jane looked at Mimi, with her serenity, her style, her obvious acceptance of her heritage and wondered how the girl she described could have turned into this woman. So she asked.

"I was forced to take a course in Chinese history in college. My father said I had to or he wouldn't keep paying my tuition. I didn't understand him; he wasn't a Chinese 'patriot' like my mom. Anyway, I took the class and I started getting interested in spite of myself because I came across mention of a scientist with my mother's family name. I asked her about him and it turned out he was her uncle. I think it was the first time I'd even wondered about her as an individual with a family other than us. She knew a lot about him and his work, and as we talked, I realized for the first time that she knew something about a lot of things and was an interesting person. It was a stunning realization. One thing led to another and I actually joined a Chinese students' club and met my husband, who is third generation in this country, but aggressively Chinese, and well—here I am," she added.

"I'd say you turned out okay," Jane said.

"Thanks." Mimi suddenly looked embarrassed about having talked about herself.

"Tell me about the others. What about Beth?"

Mimi thought for a moment. "I don't know much about her now. The others say she's a big deal, but I wasn't aware of it. She was sure an interesting person. Her mother was an over-the-hill hooker when they moved here. At least, that was the gossip. I think Beth was in about seventh grade then. Her mom had been reduced to taking in ironing to make a living."

"I thought Ewe Lambs were top drawer," Jane said.

"I guess she was the exception that proved the rule. Beth managed to disassociate herself from her mother even better than I did. Something must have clicked in her brain when she was very little. She decided to make herself Perfect, with a capital P. She was always immaculately well-groomed, a brilliant student, manners so good the rest of us looked like Neanderthals—I suppose we were, really. Somehow she managed to avoid ever being the subject of gossip. People snickered about her mother, but never about her. She had no really close friends that I know of, but no enemies. She was nice to everybody, even the geeks. She baby-sat, gave piano lessons, had a paper route before girls did such things, and, in spite of all that, had the best grades in the school. It was really amazing and admirable. Besides all that, she dated the most popular guy. Ted Francisco. Dating Ted was probably the deciding factor in her selection for the Ewe Lambs. It would have made them look silly if Judge Francisco's son's girlfriend wasn't one of us."

"Dead Ted? Oh, dear. It must be very hard for her to stay here. Were they still dating when he died?"

Mimi nodded. "Until that night."

"What do you mean?"

"She broke up with him on Prom Night. He killed himself later that evening."

"Oh, my God!"

"It must have been unspeakably horrible for her," Mimi said. "She was right, of course. She'd gotten into Stanford on a full scholarship and had already decided to be an attorney. Poor Ted barely squeaked into being accepted at a local junior college. Her mother was going to California with her. Beth and Ted were never going to cross paths again and she was sensible enough to realize they ought to make a clean break."

"And he killed himself over it! The bastard!"

Mimi nodded again. "It wasn't the popular thing to think, but it's how I felt at the time, too. What's really ironic is that he hadn't exactly been 'true' to her anyway. He'd dated Pooky before he started going with Beth and he still flirted with her like mad. She was a stunning beauty at the time, but too stupid to realize he was making a fool of her. And he was great chums with Crispy, who was a neighbor and lifelong friend of the family. Crispy was a mess of a girl then and worshiped him. There were even rumors that he was seeing a girl from another school, so nobody expected that he'd take getting dumped so badly. But then, who can tell what's in anybody else's mind? Just yesterday Lila told me that Ted's father, who was a highly respected judge, had written a great recommendation letter for Beth and helped her get into Stanford, even though I very much doubt that the Franciscos thought she was good enough for their precious son. Meanwhile poor old Ted himself couldn't even get out of town."

"It sounds like you didn't like him very well."

"Oh, I had a crush on him like everybody else at the time, even though he paid no attention to me. But no, I don't think in retrospect that I ever really *liked* him. He was spoiled and . . . well, somehow meanspirited. But that's an adult view. As a teenager, all I could see was his spectacular facade. Even Avalon—well, you saw the drawing. She hung around making little sketches of him, his car, anything to do with him."

Jane took a sip of her drink and sat back, thinking. "Shelley originally said this place would have bad associations for the Ewe Lambs. I had no idea how bad. Was anybody *not* in love with Ted Francisco?"

"Of this group? Probably not. Lila went out with him once or twice between Pooky's and Beth's reigns and later claimed she'd refused any more dates with him, but he told everybody how dull she was, so I imagine it was his choice, not hers. I think she came to actively dislike him, but it was a love-hate thing. Oh, there's Kathy. I don't think Kathy ever gave him much of a thought except to consider him part of the capitalist pig army she was devoted to eradicating. She wouldn't have gone out with any male who didn't have a beard and long hair and a dirty T-shirt with something obscene written on it."

"I know something that will surprise you about her," Jane said, and explained what she and Crispy had found in Kathy's purse. " . . . so apparently she's quite well-off," she finished the account. "I didn't mean to snoop, but when I saw the watch and ring and the checkbook with that balance . . ."

"I'd have snooped, too," Mimi said. "How fascinating."

"Crispy says the rule of reunions is that nobody is what they seem to be."

"Almost nobody," Mimi agreed. "I haven't the imagination to invent a persona for myself."

"I wonder who Crispy really is," Jane said.

Mimi laughed. "God only knows! She's deliberately put on so many layers of charming, utterly fake personality that there's no telling what's underneath."

"And Lila? Who was Lila?" Jane asked.

Kathy came slouching in and sprawled in the chair next to Jane. "Are you going to finish that sandwich? May I have it?"

"Sure, help yourself," Jane said, noticing now that the watch and ring line and condition of her hands were truly obvious when you knew to look.

"I'm telling Jane a little bit about all of us," Mimi said. "I'm trying to think how to describe Lila."

"In competition with everybody," Kathy mumbled through a big bite of sandwich.

"You're right. I never thought about it that way, but that's what was so irritating about her back in high school," Mimi said, obviously surprised at Kathy being so on-target. "Not only in competition, but thinking she was winning every round and constantly talking about her imagined victories. She had better clothes than anybody, a better hairdresser, better grades—except for Beth, of course—and far better breeding."

"All those Adamses she was always shooting off her mouth about," Kathy said, reaching over and polishing off Jane's drink.

Mimi smiled. "I remember. She was always trying to knock us out with the fact that she was related to John Adams and we couldn't have cared less. Now, if she'd been related to Mick Jagger—"

"Lila?" Kathy laughed.

Mimi went on, "Naturally, Beth drove her wild. Beth was not only genuinely better at everything, but she was gracious about it and Lila couldn't stand it. They both decided to run for president of the Ewe Lambs our senior year and when Beth found out, she withdrew, saying she didn't like to compete with a friend. Lila, of course, thought that she was being patronized and Beth really meant she didn't want to embarrass her by beating her. Which was probably true. It infuriated Lila. She was such a fool."

"Is that why she was niggling at Beth about the Supreme Court thing last night?" Jane asked.

"That and general nastiness," Mimi said. "She was really a very bitter, unhappy person. God knows why. She had every advantage you'd think anybody could want. Yes, she probably still felt she was in competition with Beth and as it looked like Beth was way out in front, she had to drag her back. I'd like to meet the person who could really find out anything bad about Beth. It's just not possible."

"Oh, I don't know. She probably has some skeleton in her closet. Everybody does," Kathy said.

"You're just saying that because she's a judge and you're a rebel," Mimi said with a smile.

"Yeah, sure I am—" Kathy sat up and looked straight at Jane. "I've been meaning to mention to you that you did a nice job of cleaning up my room. Even the contents of my purse are neat and tidy."

## 10

"I didn't want all of you to know how I'd failed," Kathy was weeping noisily five minutes later.

Mimi sat on the arm of Kathy's chair, patting her shoulder and making sympathetic noises. "You're hardly a failure, Kathy. We all grow up and change. There's nothing shameful about that. In fact, it's a good thing we don't have to stay what we were as teenagers all our lives."

"But most of you changed for the better. All I accomplished was to just marry a man who invented a gadget that made us rich. Beth's a big-deal judge, probably going to end up on the Supreme Court someday, for God's sake! Crispy got pretty and stylish and funny. You're gorgeous and happy with yourself."

"I don't mean to be catty, but there *is* Pooky," Mimi said with a smile she obviously hoped would help diffuse Kathy's emotions.

"Pooky!" Kathy snorted. "She's too stupid to walk and chew gum at the same time. Nobody'd expect anything of her. Why, even that strung-out loser Avalon's got a mob of foster kids, with handicaps yet, and she's kept her looks, too, dammit. It's not fair. All I've got is thirty extra pounds, a seven-bedroom house, and four spoiled brats. My oldest son has his own Ferrari. Hell! I should have made something of myself. Of my kids. Of the world. I wanted to, I really did. I had the brains

85

and the drive and the ideals. And then Harold patented
that damned computer hardware thing—"

"What kind of computer thing?" Jane asked.

Kathy wailed. "I don't even know! A chip conduc-
tor or a floppy cable or something stupid! At first I
tried to talk him into giving the money away. There
was so damned much of it. Set up an environmental
trust, I said. Make your name live in history. Like
Edison, but with a social conscience. But he told me
we had to think of the kids and he was right. I could
see the justice in that. So he told me if I'd invest for
them for five years, then he wouldn't object if I gave
the rest away. And so I learned all about the stock
market—"

"And you were good at it?" Jane guessed. Out of
the corner of her eye she noticed Beth had come
inside and was standing quietly by the doors to the
patio. Hector was still with her, but when he spotted
Jane, he made a beeline for her lap. He landed with
a solid thud. Jane obligingly scratched the top of
his head.

"Good at it?," Kathy said, "I'm a goddamned wiz-
ard! I couldn't lose money if I tried. I *don't* invest
in South Africa though!" She looked around at them
defiantly.

"No, of course not," Mimi murmured, smiling over
Kathy's head at Jane.

"—and pretty soon the five years had become six
and I couldn't stop. I can't even blame Harold. It
wasn't his fault. It was my own! I got greedy! I sold
out! And I'm nothing now but your average rich bitch.
I've turned into my *mother!*" Her voice rose to nearly
a shriek.

"You're hardly average, Kathy," Beth said from
where she'd been listening at the French doors. She

came in and sat down, but kept a safe distance, probably for fear of being cried on. "You don't know this, but you and I have a friend in common who's kept me up on you. He tells me that you know more about the pharmaceutical industry than anybody he's ever heard of. He says *Barron's* and the *Wall Street Journal* consult with you before they comment on medical matters."

"You knew all along?" Kathy said, smirking a little at the compliment and sniffling revoltingly into a tissue that Mimi had handed her.

"I'm afraid so."

"So did Crispy," Jane said softly. "At least she knew you were rich."

"What did she do, help you search my room?" Kathy asked nastily.

"I *wasn't* searching your room. I explained that to you." No point in adding that Crispy had, indeed, gone through her billfold. It wasn't relevant. "She knew because of your hands."

"My hands?" Kathy looked at them as if they didn't belong to her. "So damned near everybody knew. Beth, Crispy, Lila—"

"Lila knew?" Mimi asked.

"Oh, sure. That snoopy bitch knew everything. She used to be married to a private detective, she said. She bragged about how she was able to find out practically anything about anybody. Give me that cat!"

Hector allowed himself to be transferred and hugged fiercely.

"She told you this here?" Jane asked.

"Yes, yesterday afternoon," Kathy said, petting Hector in a manner that almost qualified as mauling. Hector brbrmeowed happily. "She was leading up to a little ever-so-ladylike blackmail. Her with her frumpy clothes and her DAR membership."

Jane leaned forward. "What did you tell her?"

Kathy looked genuinely surprised at the question. "I told her to fuck off. What do you think? I'm not stupid about what I do with my money."

"—and?" Jane prodded.

"And she backed off. But it was temporary. She minced about how embarrassing it would be for everybody to know my real life and how she'd just let me think about it a while and she was certain I'd see the sense in giving her a little help over a rough spot." Kathy had lapsed into imitating Lila's precise, slightly Boston accent with chilling accuracy.

"And then somebody killed the bitch," Kathy added in her own voice. "And I'm glad!"

"Kathy, that's a reckless thing to say," Beth warned her.

"It's the truth. And we're having a goddamned sloppy moment of truth here, aren't we? Well—shit! The charade's over. I'm going to take a shower and get out of these dumb clothes."

She dislodged Hector, got up, and stomped off, nearly upsetting Mimi, who was still perched on the arm of the chair. Hector ambled over to the French doors and went back outside.

Beth, Mimi, and Jane looked at each other for a long moment before Beth said softly, "Oh, dear."

Mimi and Jane started giggling from sheer nerves.

But they stopped abruptly when Pooky came into the room, still looking confused and lost. "I'm sorry to interrupt you," she said.

"You're not," Beth said. "What's wrong?"

"Well, I hate to say this, but my room's been ransacked and something's missing," she cast a half-apologetic glance at Jane.

"Ransacked! Well, my cleaning skills aren't too

good, but they're not *that* bad. Besides, I didn't ever get to your room," Jane assured her. "What's missing?"

"It's this antique pen thingie. It's very valuable. One of the guys in our class saw it when he was in my town and he didn't buy it, but then he saw my address in the roster and asked me to bring it to him at the reunion. He sent them a check and I just picked it up. I guess he didn't trust the mail. The price tag was still taped to the bottom. It cost five thousand dollars and now it's missing. I don't know what to do!" She burst into tears, which pulled her poor face in odd directions and made her look not quite human.

"This is going too far!" Mimi said, showing real anger for the first time. "The only people who have left this house today are Jane and Crispy and they couldn't have sneaked it out without the other one noticing." She glanced at Jane. "Not that either of you *would* steal anything. So it's got to be in this house someplace and we're going to find it. Everybody is going to help!"

The "antique pen thingie" turned up, unharmed, in an otherwise empty wastebasket in the utility room, but not before Pooky had full-fledged hysterics and the rest of the searchers came to harsh words several times. Shelley had called a short meeting to deliver a fierce little lecture on the stupidity of playing these jokes and everybody agreed, even though it was obvious that one of them was, in fact, the perpetrator.

Edgar had taken three aspirins and gone upstairs to take a nap to kill his headache. He expressed the opinion that he'd rather kill himself, just at the moment. It was a remark that didn't go over very well. Jane soothed as many ruffled feathers as she could and then had gone from room to room collecting glasses, dishes, and dirty ashtrays. She'd just finished washing them when the phone rang. She lunged for it before it could disturb Edgar's much-needed rest.

"Bed and breakfast," she answered.

"Jane? I'm glad you answered."

"Mel?"

"Can you get away for a few minutes? I'm coming over there. But I want to talk to you before I come in."

Jane glanced at her watch and quickly reviewed her schedule. She was due to drive a car pool in fifteen minutes, then she was free until five, when she was coming back to help with dinner. Then she was off again to attend Back-To-School night. "I'm only free for a few minutes if you get here right away."

"I'm just down the street and what I have to tell you will only take a minute."

Jane dashed to let Shelley know she was leaving. She found her friend in the library, slamming folders around and trying to organize the notes of her aborted morning meeting. "Why did you let me do this!" Shelley said coldly.

"Stars in your crown. The Goddess of Entertaining is looking down on you even as we speak and giving you full credit. I'm off. See you at five."

Mel was parked at the far end of the drive by the gates. Jane got in his little red MG and said, "So?"

He took a deep breath. "There were two people in the carriage house. Two different sets of fingerprints."

"Can you identify them?"

"We don't need to. They turned themselves in an hour ago."

"Mel! That's wonderful! It's over. You've solved it. Why do you look like last night's pizza?"

"The beer and cigarettes belonged to two thirteen-year-old boys who'd sneaked out of their houses for a big thrill. They each had a beer and a cigarette and were starting to feel kind of sick before their eyes adjusted to the dark and they realized they were sitting a few feet from a dead body."

"Oh. . . ."

"They came to the station with their parents. They heard about it on the noon news."

"And you believe them?"

Mel sighed. "Jane, one of the poor kids wet his pants right there in my office he was so scared. The mothers were in hysterics. One of the fathers started crying. It was awful! And it's the God's truth, I'd swear to it. I've met a lot of guilty people and a few innocent ones and I'd stake my reputation on the fact that they're innocent. They were terrified. The one kept saying he'd never seen a dead body before, even when his grandmother died. I turned them over to a psychologist. The whole gang of them. Parents, everybody. The lab will do tests on their clothes and so forth, but there's no doubt in my mind."

Jane looked back at the house. She saw a curtain on the third floor twitch. Edgar—or Gordon—watching. "When were they there?"

"About midnight, they think."

"So she was dead by then."

Mel nodded.

"And—?"

He looked straight at her. "And it looks like we're going to have to know a whole lot more about the people staying here."

Jane knew perfectly well what he meant, but she needed to hear him say it. "You don't really think one of those women killed her?"

"Probably," he said bluntly. "I need to know about them."

Jane glanced at her watch. "I don't know much, but there isn't time to tell you what I do know. I have to pick up kids at school."

He took her hand, but it was an absentminded gesture, not an affectionate one. "I didn't mean right now. We've got people doing background checks. What I need to know now is the schedule for this meeting. Nobody thinks they're leaving soon, do they?"

"No. The actual reunion starts tomorrow. Mel, I have to leave. What are you going to do?"

"I'm going to explain this to the owners and guests, give official warnings about not leaving, and set up a watch on the house."

"Mel—"

"Yes?"

"Well, it's just odd. . . . of all the women attending the meeting, the only one nasty enough to imagine casting as a murderer was the one who got killed. They're nice women, Mel."

"One of them's not."

# — 11 —

Jane ran her car pool on autopilot while her mind leaped around the facts and impressions jumbling in her mind. She'd have to organize her recollections before she passed them on to Mel. One thing seemed clear: Lila was a blackmailer. And if she'd tried it out on Kathy, she'd probably tried it out on others. All those nasty little digs she'd made the evening before were probably references to threats she'd already made or was paving the way to make later. The story she'd told suggesting that Avalon had experimented with drugs in high school was probably such an attempt. What else had she said? There had been a remark to Pooky about having a real understanding of the psychology of teenaged boys. What had that been about? Pooky had looked either stricken or confused by it, with the oddities of her facial expression, it was hard to tell which.

"Mom! You forgot to let off Jason," her son Todd said as they pulled into their own driveway.

"Oh, no I didn't," Jane said with a laugh. "I just like Jason so much I wanted to bring him home with us." She backed out and headed for Jason's house. Todd was looking mortally embarrassed by his mother's feeble joke.

When they got home the second time, there was a crisis. Mike had spilled a glass of orange juice all over a stack of his college applications and they had to dash back to school and beat the doors down to get in to acquire duplicates. Back home yet again, Jane had to cope with Katie, whose snit with her friend Jenny had escalated to nasty phone calls and hanging up on each other.

"I'm going to tell everybody everything I know about Jenny!" Katie exclaimed. "Like about how she had to go to the doctor because she wet the bed—"

Jane's patience, already at low ebb, disappeared entirely. "No, you're not!" she said. "You're going to behave like a lady. Those are friendship secrets and if the friendship dies, the secrets die with it."

Katie looked stunned at this outburst.

"Katie, I mean it. You'll regret it the rest of your life if you tell Jenny's secrets. Other people might like knowing the secrets, but they won't like you for telling them. And you'll never really, really like *yourself* again."

Katie fidgeted with her hair and looked out the window. "How do you know?"

"Because I'm a grown-up and I'm smarter than you," Jane said, uttering the one phrase she had sworn she would never use. She'd never succumbed to it before today, but she was rattled by the events at the bed and breakfast.

"Look Katie, I'm sorry I said that, but it *is* true. I've had experience in all kinds of things that you haven't yet. And I want to keep you from making big mistakes. It's my job as a mother to make sure you don't harm your opinion of yourself. Do you understand?"

To her astonishment, Katie hugged her hard and ran upstairs without a word.

Jane sat down at the kitchen table, shaking her head.

All those years she'd spent trying to explain, cajole, and gently urge Katie along, and this time a firm order had not only worked, but elicited a rare expression of affection. Why didn't they issue a handbook in the delivery room that explained which approach would work when? And why was it so hard for mothers and daughters to get along? Her boys were easy. They seemed genuinely to like her most of the time and if they disagreed with her rules, they criticized the rules, not her character. It must have to do with hormones, she concluded unhappily.

She threw together a quick dinner for the kids, gave last warnings about house rules while she was gone, and dashed back to the bed and breakfast to help Edgar. He was planning an elaborate dinner that night of glazed ham steaks with raisin/ginger sauce, julienned potatoes fried into tiny baskets with an artichoke heart filling, and a salad with a thousand finely diced ingredients. This was in addition to a raspberry soufflé for dessert and rolls that had to be watched carefully. He and Jane were so busy with the dinner itself that there was little time for chat about anything else. The only reference to murder was when Edgar said, "Would you prepare a tray for what's his name to eat in the library?"

"Which what's his name?"

"The officer they've left here to keep an eye on things." Edgar said this so bitterly that Jane didn't ask any other questions.

When everything was nearly ready to serve, Edgar said, "Gordon will help me take everything in. You run along to your meeting."

Jane glanced at her watch with horror. The Back-To-School night was starting in five minutes and she had to be there on time or she'd be assigned all kinds of responsibilities she didn't want. It was highly dangerous to miss this night because the nonattendees, as a punishment, were given hideous jobs in their absence.

Jane got off lucky. No driving on field trips, no fund-raising carnival jobs, no baking for PTA meetings. Only assistant room mother for the Christmas—to be politically correct, Winter Break—party. It would be unspeakably horrible, of course, but it was still a couple of months away and the head room mother under whom she would work was a bossy woman who always ran the whole thing herself anyway. Jane even managed to protect Shelley from being voted PTA secretary, for which Shelley would owe her at least another permanent.

When she returned to the bed and breakfast very early the next morning, she discovered that Shelley's personality had come back up to full force the evening before and she had compelled the other women to tend to the business of having their fund-raising meeting. God only knew how she had done it. Jane suspected it would be generations before the meeting faded from the collective minds of Ewe Lamb history. She told Shelley so.

Shelley was tidying up the last of her paperwork in the kitchen, packing it away into file folders. "I got a call a while ago about buying the rights to do a Movie of the Week about it. They've run out of diseases and are going into severe personality disorders," she said, collapsing into a chair. "I've never been so tired in my life, Jane."

"This might perk you up. That vicious Elaine person you fell out with over the carnival budget tried to nominate you for secretary of the PTA."

"The bitch!" Shelley said, horrified.

"Don't worry. I put a stick in her spokes. But I couldn't save you from directing the 'Brownies Around the World' program for the Spring Fling."

Shelley waved that away. "Piece of cake. They're all children. It's the adults I can't stand working with. Secretary. The nerve. She'll regret this." She levered herself out of the chair. "I'm through hostessing. I'm going home and take a bath in my own bathroom and a long nap. After beating up someone."

"Anyone in particular?"

"My sister-in-law Constanza."

"The unmarried one who's watching your kids?"

"The unmarried, snoopy one. I locked all our personal papers and my jewelry in that safe I had put in the linen closet last month. She's probably had in locksmiths by now. She loves pawing through our stuff and then making inventories for the rest of Paul's brothers and sisters. She's probably made a list of how many bras I—Oh! How could I forget? Go take a look at the living room."

"The Joker again?"

"And how!"

Jane opened the door cautiously and didn't know whether to be shocked or to laugh at the sight. The room was festooned with underwear. Bras draped over lampshades, panties suspended from television knobs and drawer handles, slips hanging over the coffee table, pantyhose spread-eagled on the sofa.

Jane closed the door and came back into the kitchen. "Crispy's?"

"Probably. Part of it anyway. You'll have to take a closer look later. Some of the stuff is *real* raunchy. Crotchless panties with obscene sayings, bras with the nipples cut out. The embroidered phrase 'Tuesday's

Tits' sticks in my mind. If she really brought that stuff along, she was expecting this reunion to be a lot more fun that most of us were anticipating."

"Where was the cop they left here while this was being done?"

"Probably asleep on the sofa in the library. He'll probably be in big trouble for not apprehending somebody, even though it's not a crime to redecorate with lingerie."

"Does Edgar know? Poor Edgar."

"No, but I think he's beyond caring. I believe Gordon's really worried about his state of mind. He stayed home today, too."

A shriek of laughter came from the other room as someone else discovered the underwear. "This trick's odd, Shelley," Jane said. "It seems more elaborate. More personal. It seems to actually 'mean' something."

Shelley picked up her purse. "I'm too tired to analyze the fine points. I'll be back later. Or maybe I'll just go to the airport and ask them to put me on the next plane leaving the country."

As Shelley left, Edgar came into the kitchen. If Gordon was worried about him, he shouldn't have been. Edgar looked rested and relaxed. "Jane! You're bright and early," he said, opening the door to the mammoth refrigerator.

"Edgar, you're so perky!"

"I think I'll do the creamed eggs and asparagus this morning," he said. "Yes. Over toast points. Maybe a breath of curry . . ."

He was back on form. As Jane made the basic white sauce for him and was inordinately pleased when he complimented her on it, Crispy came in the kitchen, her eyes red and her voice trembling. "Where is the wastebasket?" she said, holding out a wad of flamboyantly colored underwear as if it were soiled.

"Over there," Edgar gestured. "What's that?"

"Disgusting underwear," Crispy said. "A nasty, filthy little trick."

She was genuinely upset, which surprised Jane. In the back of her mind, Jane had been assuming that Crispy herself was the Joker. She hadn't even consciously realized this before now. But obviously this wasn't a joke Crispy had played on herself to avoid suspicion. This joke had really bothered her. Jane kept stirring the sauce, turning the heat down slightly. It was possible, though, that Crispy had played the other tricks, and someone else—suspecting her—had engineered this one. It was difficult enough to imagine that this group contained one practical joker, let alone two.

Jane had a desperate craving to just sit down and think for a long time. These last two days had dumped so much information, and so many impressions into her, that her subconscious seemed to have sunk under the weight of them. She was sorry that she and Shelley couldn't sit out on the patio, or at one of their kitchen tables, and chew it over together. They were such good, familiar friends that they could communicate in a verbal shorthand that was very comfortable. And sometimes very productive.

Edgar took over the sauce and Jane went to the dining room to set the table. Most of the women had gathered there and were standing around the silver coffee urn. They were discussing the fund-raising activities that had been decided on the evening before. Shelley would have been pleased.

As preoccupied as she was, Jane couldn't help but notice the change in Kathy. Instead of the dreadful hick/hippy clothes she'd been wearing before, she had on a very smart, crisp plaid blouse and neat denim skirt. This preppy, casual outfit even included a colorful woven belt, hose, and apparently some very effective underpinnings that did wonders for her rather generous figure. She was still a big woman, but a very tidy big woman.

Mimi and Beth were still in robes, albeit a very elegant black silk robe that would have done as a hostess gown in Mimi's case. Beth, in a tailored blue robe that looked utterly sexless, had gone remote, as if she'd fully realized that this wasn't a good place for a woman who had to maintain an impeccably orderly public life to be.

Avalon, in jeans and an elaborately knitted beige sweater with beads and what appeared to be twigs woven in, had really gotten into the fund-raising spirit and was chattering with Pooky about a craft booth someplace. They were deeply involved in the theoretical pricing of tie-dyed scarves. Crispy was still sulking.

Jane went back to the kitchen to eat. Gordon and Edgar were at the kitchen table, where they'd set a place for her and the policeman, who'd apparently heard about the practical joke with the underwear and was looking distinctly worried. Gordon was studying a piece of paper. "It's very clever, isn't it? Look at all the details."

"What's that?" Jane asked.

"One of the women gave Edgar this picture," he said, turning it so she could see.

"Oh, Avalon's drawing of the carriage house. I thought Pooky had probably gotten it away from her. It is clever. That was nice of her to give it to you."

"I'll get it framed next week. A deep gray mat with

a narrow black frame, I believe," Gordon said. "Where do you think it should go?"

"Upstairs for now," Edgar said, "if one of the guests is hot to get her hands on it. These women are really odd."

Echoing Mel, Jane said, "No, not all of them. Only one."

## 12

"Where's Shelley today?" Crispy asked from the kitchen doorway.

"She's gone home for a while—to punch out her sister-in-law, probably," Jane answered, stacking the last of the breakfast plates in the dishwasher.

"And what's become of Edgar?"

"He needed a few things from the grocery store. I told him to go on and I'd clean up."

"Want some help?"

"No, but I'd love company. There's some coffee left, if you'd like."

Crispy poured herself a cup and sat down with it and a cigarette. "Want one?"

"When I'm done," Jane said. "I'm trying to cut down to six a day. But I went off the rails last night and smoked four in a row because I couldn't sleep."

"I wish I could stop entirely," Crispy said.

"Unfortunately, it takes more than wishing," Jane replied.

"Listen, I'm sorry I was such an ass this morning about the underwear. It was just such a nasty trick and it really embarrassed me."

Jane put a dishcloth in the bottom of the sink and laid the crystal juice glasses on their sides on it before running hot water over them. "Crispy, answer me honestly, okay? Haven't you been the one playing the tricks?"

"God's truth, no!"

Jane poured dishwashing soap over the glasses and began to wash them. "But when I first met you, you implied that you were here just to cause trouble."

"Yes, but it soon became apparent to me that Lila was going to cause quite enough without any help from me," Crispy said wryly.

"But Lila wasn't responsible for the underwear. Or that antique thing of Pooky's being stolen and hidden."

"No. . . ."

"Then who do you think it is playing the tricks?"

"I really haven't the faintest idea. Mimi, maybe?"

"Surely not! She was really angry about that thing of Pooky's being taken. She's the one who made everybody look for it."

"How do you know that wasn't a good act?" Crispy asked. "She's quite an actress, you know. Always had the lead in the school plays. We did *Oklahoma* our junior year and she played the goody-two-shoes role. Five minutes into it, you forgot all about her Chinese features and believed she was that girl. She played Lady Macbeth just as well."

"Is that so?" Jane said. That was interesting information, and put her conversation with Mimi the previous afternoon in a whole different light. Jane had accepted everything Mimi had said about the others without question. Maybe she should get a second opinion.

"Tell me about the others," she said, carefully rinsing the crystal glasses and setting them on the counter on a dry towel.

"The kind version or the catty version?"

"Have you got two versions for everybody?"

Crispy laughed. "No, I've only got the catty version. Well, you know everything I know about Kathy."

"I mean what they were really like in high school. Not now."

"Kathy in high school—hmmm, a spoiled rich girl with too much energy and intelligence, looking for something to focus it on that would make people pay attention to her and drive her parents crazy at the same time. She had attention and respect and love all mixed up and thought they were the same thing."

Jane finished with the glasses and came to sit down at the kitchen table with Crispy, who pushed a leather cigarette case and silver lighter toward her. "You've thought about them a lot, haven't you?" Jane said, taking a long drag.

"I did then. You probably won't believe this, but I was really shy and insecure then."

"Come on."

"I was. I thought I was the most boring person in the world—which was probably quite true—and so I paid a lot of attention to everybody else. Trying to decide which one of them I wanted to be when I grew up, I guess. Living a vicarious life through the others. I did have the sense, thank God, to know I didn't want to be Kathy, though."

"Who *did* you want to be?"

"Either Beth or Lila," Crispy answered without hesitation. "That's odd, considering the way Lila turned out, but I did admire her then. She was a snooty little bitch, but she carried it off with style. Sort of like a young Katharine Hepburn. She always wore clothes that looked like they were hand-me-downs from a maiden aunt, but she wore them with such self-assurance that I envied her. I thought she seemed much more mature than the rest of us. I suppose it was really only discontent, but it seemed like sophistication to me."

"You admired her more than Beth?"

"Not more. Just in a different way. Beth was absolutely perfect, but sort of remote, without any interesting sharp edges. Like she was always concentrating very hard on not turning into her mother. Poor Mrs. Vaughn, if she *was* a 'Mrs.' She tried so hard to fit in for Beth's sake. Came to all the Mother's Meetings and things, but always with too much makeup and clouds of cheap perfume and a voice a little too shrill. Beth was the kind of girl who probably didn't dare make very close friends with anybody because then she'd have to let them come to her house like friends do. And that might have wrecked her ambitions. Still, I admired her style and grace and brains."

"What about Pooky? What was she like?"

"Dim as a twenty-five-watt bulb. But gorgeous. You'd never know it now, but she was really stunning. The kind of person that strangers in the street stop to look at with amazement and admiration."

"I know. I saw her picture in the yearbook."

"—but *so* stupid. I had a whole slew of stories saved up to embarrass her with, but when I saw her ruined face, I just didn't have the heart. I was prepared to deflate her vanity, but life's done that to her already. She was the kind of person they tell dumb blond jokes about now. The boys were crazy about her. Naturally. She was a pretty good athlete, too. She could run like the wind, and do acrobatics, and dance. She was head cheerleader and Prom Queen, but you could have used her skull to drain lettuce. It must have been devastating to her to lose her looks, with nothing to fall back on like brains or skills or personality. It's actually pretty brave of her to have come to the reunion. She's actually quite a nice woman now that she's not beautiful."

"Watch it," Jane said. "Your cattiness is slipping."

Crispy grinned and lighted another cigarette. "Then let's talk about Avalon. That'll bring it back."

"You didn't like her?"

"What was to like? She was an egotistical wimp. Still is. She sort of crept around like a morbid shadow, drawing her oh-so-precious little pictures, looking like she was always on the brink of tears. She was the kind of shy person who's totally self-absorbed, always seeing reasons to get their feelings hurt and imagining that people are talking about them when nobody even knows who they are. And she loved the opportunity to be the martyr. She's still doing it. Didn't you hear her going on and on about all her dear little handicapped foster children?"

"How come she got into the Ewe Lambs? I thought they were a pretty exclusive group. She doesn't sound like she fit the image."

"She didn't, but every year they had to have a token artsy-fartsy person. That was to give the illusion of democracy. Sort of like having a bulldog as a pet— to suggest that you could look beneath the surface appearances. She nearly drove Ted crazy." Crispy suddenly fell silent.

"Ted—?" Jane said encouragingly.

Crispy looked away. "Ted was my friend. My only real friend," she said. "We grew up together, like a brother and sister. He was an only child and so was I. All the others were after him as a boyfriend, a date that would give them status. They were all using him, even Beth. Especially Beth. But I was the one he talked to, really talked to. I sometimes think that if he hadn't died, he and I might have eventually—

well, that's stupid. He did die, the son of a bitch!"

"I'm surprised you don't hate Beth," Jane said.

"Oh, you've heard the story about how she broke his poor, fragile heart and he couldn't face life, huh? Well, he didn't kill himself over her," Crispy said.

"No?"

"No. He didn't care that much for her anymore. The bloom had gone off the rose, as they say. He knew she was only dating him because of his dad, because of the judge's status in the legal community."

*Or so you'd like to believe,* Jane thought.

"No, whatever the reason was, it wasn't Beth."

"Then what was it?"

"I've never known. I'm not so sure he *did* commit suicide, not deliberately."

"How do you mean?"

"Well, they'd broken up at the prom. He probably was pretty shocked and insulted that she'd dumped him before he got around to dumping her. He got drunk and angry and came home. I think maybe he just meant to come home for a while—maybe go back over to her house later and tell her off or something. Or maybe come over and talk to me about it. Anyway, he could have left the car engine running and gone upstairs to get something. And if he changed his mind, and forgot about the car or just passed out . . ."

"But didn't Avalon say she was drawing the carriage house when she heard the car engine *start?* Remember, when she was showing us the picture she brought along? She said she'd done it that night."

"Oh, she was just being melodramatic," Crispy said. "And even if she did hear him start the car, the same thing could hold true. He came home for something, started to leave and remembered something else he wanted to go back upstairs for."

"I've got to get on with my jobs," Jane said. She'd suddenly heard all she could stand to hear about Dead Ted. The thought of a teenaged boy, the same age as her own Mike, dying, by accident or on purpose, was too depressing to contemplate.

"I'm sorry. I've offended you."

"No, you haven't," Jane assured her. "It's just that I promised Edgar I'd help him and he'll be back any minute. I need to get busy."

"Thanks for listening. I'm sorry I unloaded on you." She laughed. "You weren't one of the ones I intended to come here to punish for not recognizing my sterling qualities when I was a fat, seventeen-year-old lump."

"Is that why you came to the reunion?"

"Pretty much so. But someone else seems to have usurped my role as dispenser of overdue justice."

"You mean killing Lila?"

"Lila—and all the tricks."

"If you had to guess—" Jane began.

"I wouldn't guess," Crispy said firmly. "And a smart person like you won't either. It could be a dangerous game."

It wasn't until she was ascending the stairs with her cleaning materials that Jane remembered that she meant to ask Crispy what had been in Lila's note-book.

## 13

Pooky had just started cleaning up her room when Jane arrived to do it. "Go on, visit with your friends," Jane said. "I'll do this for you."

"Let me help you. I'd rather. They're all in Kathy's room, talking about politics and things. I'm not as clever as everybody else on that stuff."

"Then let's start with the bed," Jane said. "I've got fresh sheets here. I think I'd prefer to miss a political discussion with Kathy, too. I don't blame you."

"It's not that I don't know about other things," Pooky said, taking off the bedspread and folding it with excruciating neatness even though they were going to put it right back on the bed. "I used to be a travel agent and I went lots of places. Acapulco, Hawaii, the French Riviera . . ."

*The culture meccas,* Jane thought.

"Have you been to those places?" Pooky asked.

"Some of them. My father is with the State Department and I grew up all over the world. I've lived in about seventeen different countries."

"Then you know what I mean. You can't travel without learning a lot. But I've never liked that stuff Kathy is always talking about. It just depresses me. Like nature programs. I used to really like nature programs—about penguins and flowers and things—

but now when you watch them, they just make you feel awful. They're always all about how terrible people are ruining things. Oil spills and ozone and rain forests. I mean, what can *I* do about it? They never tell you that. They just make you feel horrible, then there's a commercial."

Jane looked at her with surprise. "You know . . . you're right!" She didn't mean to sound quite so astonished.

But Pooky didn't take offense. "Kathy's like that. She's always mad about people who aren't doing the right thing, but she doesn't talk about what the right thing is. She was always like that. Against stuff instead of for anything. I mean, what good is that?"

"So she hasn't changed since high school?"

"No, nobody has really. Except Mimi. Isn't she beautiful?"

"She sure is."

"She was real cute in school, too. But she's grown up real nice. Peaceful and polite. She was sort of wild and—I don't know the word—"

"Frenzied?" Jane guessed.

Pooky was pleased. "Yes, that's it. That's what I meant."

"What about Avalon? Has she changed?" Jane asked, putting new cases on the pillows while Pooky made hospital corners on the sheets.

"Oh, not at all. Avalon's wonderful. She's so talented. Did you see that picture she drew of the carriage house? Wasn't that fantastic? I hoped she'd give it to me, but I guess she didn't understand how much I liked it and she gave it to that man Edgar who owns this house. I wonder if I asked him—"

"I don't think I would if I were you. He showed it to me this morning. He loves it."

"Oh, that's too bad. Well, maybe she'll make another one for me. Avalon's really nice, too. That's what's great about her. Did you know she's got foster children. She takes handicapped ones that nobody else wants."

"I'd heard that. Was she so nice in school?"

"Well, I don't know. I don't remember her all that well, except that we had a home ec class together. She was really quiet, see, and I was real popular and busy. But in home ec she made this fantastic dress. It was all sort of scraps of fabric, you know, like pretty little rags, sort of here and there. She didn't even have a pattern, can you believe it? Greens and blues and purples. I think there were some ribbons, too—she should have gone into fashion design. Now, *that's* a great field. She'd have been famous if she'd done that."

Jane smiled. Kathy wanted Avalon to use her talents to better the world; Pooky wanted her to better the state of fashion. "What does Avalon do, besides take care of the children?"

"She has a little craft store down in the Ozarks. She sells things that ladies there make, plus her own things. Quilts and like that."

"Somebody said she did drugs," Jane said. Actually both Lila and Kathy had suggested it.

Pooky nearly dropped the bedspread she'd picked back up. "No! I can't believe that anybody'd think a thing like that! I'll bet it was Lila who said that. Lila is—was—a big liar."

"Here, let's put that spread back. Lila seems to have threatened a couple of people. Did she threaten you?"

Pooky gave the spread a fierce flap and, as it settled into place, said, "No! No, there's nothing to threaten me about." Her ruined face was set in harsh lines and her hands were trembling. It was obviously a lie.

Jane's curiosity was overridden by guilt. "I'm sorry. I didn't mean to upset you."

"You didn't! I'm not upset! Now, where are the towels? Oh, I see. I'll put these away. And give me some of that cleaner stuff!"

She stomped into the bathroom and Jane could hear her crashing around, although how she did any crashing armed primarily with towels was a mystery in itself.

Jane dragged the vacuum in from the hall and shoved it around until Pooky came back out. "I'm really sorry," Jane repeated. "It must be hard on you, staying here where Ted lived. Somebody told me you dated him." She figured this line served the dual purpose of giving Pooky an excuse to be nervy and might also elicit some interesting information.

She was right on the first. Pooky fell on the justification as if it were a life raft. "It *is* strange to be here. I really hadn't thought about Ted much for the last few years and now I keep remembering him all the time. He was really a neat guy. Smart and *so* good-looking! Captain of the football team and president of the Latin Club. That was a prestigious thing, the Latin Club. I don't think kids take Latin these days. Just as well. I never did get why anybody'd care about a language you couldn't talk in. But I bet Ted could have talked it if he wanted to."

"Did you date him for a long time?" Jane asked. She wound up the vacuum cleaner cord.

"Most of our sophomore year. And part of our junior year. Then Ted—well, *we*—decided it would be better to date other people, too. It was the right decision. I mean, we were just kids, after all." But all these years later the pain was still in her voice.

"Then he dated Lila—" Jane said.

"Oh, just a couple of times. She was such a cold fish, though. Always criticizing other people. Guys don't like that, you know. They like a girl who's cheerful and fun, not somebody who's always whining and complaining. No, mainly he dated Beth."

"Mainly? Did you two still go out together?"

"Sometimes," Pooky hedged. "But I didn't want Beth to know. It would have hurt her feelings. And I wouldn't have done that for the world."

"You liked Beth?"

"We were best friends. She had her jobs and her studying and I had my cheerleading. That took a lot of time. But we spent all the time we could together." This was so unlikely as to be impossible, but apparently Pooky had convinced herself it was true.

Pooky picked up the bottle of window cleaner and spritzed it on the mirror. Jane noticed that Pooky managed to clean the mirror without looking into it. She was a brave person, like Crispy said, Jane realized. She found herself thinking, *brains aren't everything*.

"But you must have been awfully upset when Ted killed himself because she broke up with him."

Pooky laughed. "Oh, he didn't kill himself over her."

"Then what was it? Why did he do it?"

Pooky turned, looking troubled. "I don't know. I never could figure it out. Maybe he just couldn't stand it that we were all growing up and going away. Or maybe he was just drunk and feeling sorry for himself. Everybody feels sorry for themselves sometimes. I don't know."

"Crispy thinks it might have been an accident, not suicide," Jane said, starting to gather up her cleaning equipment.

"An accident? But how? Oh, like he didn't mean to start the car then go back upstairs? I don't see how. But maybe—that would be wonderful if it was an accident. I mean, not wonderful, but not so bad."

"Did you know Crispy well in school?"

"Not really well. But I liked her, I guess. Well, I was a little jealous of her, I admit. She and Ted were really good friends. Just friends, I mean, he wouldn't have dated her. She was too fat and sloppy-looking. She really was a mess. I tried to tell her once if she'd go on a diet and stop biting her nails, I'd help her with her hair and stuff, but she nearly bit my head off. She's certainly improved. She looks real stylish now. She probably could do better with her hair. That windblown look is real passé, but it's good with her face shape."

Jane smiled to herself. It was such an irony that Pooky, whose appearance was little short of frightening, always came back to people's looks and fashion sense. Inside herself someplace, she was still the high school knockout. And it was a good thing, probably the only thing that kept her going from one day to the next, one mirror to the next.

Jane touched Pooky's thin arm lightly and smiled. "Thanks for helping me. I've really enjoyed getting a chance to talk to you."

"Thanks. I like talking to you, too. You listen to me. Not many people do. I'm not as stupid as people think." Before Jane could even begin framing a tactful reply to this, Pooky went on, "And I'm going to help you with the rest of the rooms, Jane."

"Pooky, that's very generous of you, but there's no need. I don't mind doing it myself."

"If I don't help you, I'll have to go back to Kathy's room," Pooky said with a grin.

"Okay, I get it. Then let's do Avalon next."

Pooky pushed the vacuum cleaner along the hall as Jane led the way with the rest of the equipment. Jane tapped on Avalon's door and, getting no answer, opened it.

It looked like a tornado had gone through. Clothes were strewn everywhere, drawers gaped open. The dressing table was pulled out from the wall, pictures were hanging crooked, and the top half of the mattress was halfway off the bed.

Jane stopped so suddenly that Pooky ran the vacuum into the back of her foot. "Jane, I'm sor—oh, my God. What happened here?" Pooky whispered.

"Pooky, run down and peek in Kathy's room. See if Avalon's still in there." If Avalon was in *this* room, she was in trouble and Jane didn't want to be the discoverer of any more bodies. She watched Pooky, heart pounding, as she tiptoed down the hall and looked in the partly open door. Jane finally breathed when Pooky looked back and nodded.

She came back and the two of them went into the room. "What's happening here?" Pooky asked, her voice shaking.

"I don't know, but it's something nasty. This isn't a joke," Jane said, hearing a quaver in her own voice.

Just then, they heard a scream from the next room.

# — 14 —

They could smell the problem before they saw it. The scream had come from Beth's room and Jane and Crispy nearly collided as they ran toward the room from opposite directions. A horrible, skunklike smell was already wafting into the hall.

The room was empty, but the smell was so intense it almost knocked Jane out of the room. She took a deep breath and plunged back in. Beth was shrieking and pounding on the bathroom door from the inside. Jane, heart pounding wildly, tried to open the door but it was locked.

"Unlock the door!" she shouted, trying not to retch. "Calm down! Just turn the little knob." Oh, God, if she could just get one clean breath of air!

They heard Beth frantically scrabbling at the door, then suddenly it flew open and Beth stumbled out, nearly knocking Jane over.

Jane was hard on her heels.

The others gathered in the hall attempted to approach Beth, but reeled back immediately. The smell was coming from her. "In my deodorant," Beth gasped.

She was wrapped in a big towel and had another around her wet hair. She was sort of backing in circles, trying to get away from herself.

Crispy grabbed her arm and started giving orders.

"Jane, open the windows. The one in her room first. Everybody, go open your windows! Beth, come to my room and get in the shower quickly. Wash the stuff off, for God's sake!"

Avalon and Kathy were already bolting for their own rooms, gagging. Breathing through her mouth, Jane plunged into Beth's room and flung open the window. It was a cool morning and she gulped the air as if she'd nearly drowned. Then she ran back into the hall and started opening other bedroom doors to get to the windows. Within moments, she had everything open.

"What on earth—" Edgar said from the top of the stairs. "What in hell is that stink!"

"Another joke, Edgar," Jane said. "If you have an attic fan, you might want to turn it on until we get the smell out. And bring me a plastic bag, would you?"

Jane picked up a handful of cleaning rags and went first to Crispy's room. The shower was running, foul-smelling steam was pouring out the half-open bathroom door, and Crispy, standing outside it with her hand over her nose, was saying, "Use all the soap you can find. Pour the whole bottle of shampoo over yourself if you have to. It's getting better. It really is."

Jane went back to Beth's room and, taking another deep breath, went into the bathroom. The offending deodorant, the kind with liquid and a rolling ball for application, was on the bathroom floor where Beth had thrown it down. Hector had found it and was sniffing at it as if it were merely a mildly interesting odor. "Hector! Get away from that thing!" she said, shoving him out the door. Then she flung herself at the plastic bottle, capped it, and wrapped it in several layers of cleaning rags. Jane returned again to Crispy's room, Hector trying to trip her the whole way. The smell had diminished somewhat. "Is she okay?" Jane asked Crispy.

Crispy looked pale and stricken. "I think so."

Edgar knocked at the bedroom door before poking his arm into the room. He was holding the plastic bag Jane had asked for. Jane tossed the whole wad of deodorant bottle and rags into the bag. "Triple bag it, Edgar, or it'll stink up the whole neighborhood."

"What is it?"

"A trick with deodorant."

"Somebody *used* it? Smelling like this?"

"I imagine she just unscrewed it and took a quick swipe before the smell hit her. I think you better report this to the police. It could be harmful. Poison or something."

"No, don't!" Beth shouted from behind the bathroom door. The shower had stopped running. "It's just a foul odor. I'm perfectly all right."

"You're sure?" Edgar called to her.

"Absolutely sure."

"Edgar, before you decide, come look at Avalon's room," Jane said.

"All right, start from the beginning," Mel said.

Mel had said he would take an official report from Edgar in a moment, but first wanted to speak to Jane privately. They were in the driveway, sitting in his car where they couldn't be overheard. Jane was still gasping the fresh air as if she'd never smelled it before and wondering if she'd ever get the lingering odor out of her hair and clothing. Mel wasn't getting too close. She'd made some rough notes while waiting for him to arrive and consulted them. "First, Pooky's and Avalon's purse contents were exchanged. I told you about that earlier."

"Anything missing or tampered with?"

"Apparently not."

"When did this happen?"

"The day they got here. Wednesday afternoon some-time. The next thing was the alarm clocks overnight. Cheap wind-up ones had been hidden in people's rooms and set to go off every couple of hours. I think I told you about that, too."

"Who got them?" Mel asked wearily.

"Beth, Mimi, and Kathy."

"Okay, nobody hurt. No property damage," Mel said as he made a note. "Next?"

"I guess the next thing was the doorknobs. Appar-ently there's a screw in the outside half that holds it together. Somebody took the screws out of a couple, so that when the people in the rooms tried to open the doors, the doorknobs and the shafts came away in their hands."

"Could have been dangerous if there had been a fire," Mel said. "But not inherently dangerous."

"The doorknobs turned up in a flour canister in the kitchen. Along with all the screws," Jane added. "So there was no real damage done. I guess the next thing was that Crispy's underwear disappeared. Sometime while the police were here yesterday morning."

"Did she find it?"

"Oh, yes," Jane told him about the display of it in the living room, with the additional items added.

"So, nothing really stolen that wasn't returned. No property damage. Next?"

"Pooky's room was searched and messed up and an antique pen set that she was bringing along to another classmate was stolen. We found it in a wastebasket, unharmed. No property damage," she said before he could.

"Next?"

"Avalon's room was wrecked this morning."

"Wrecked?"

"No, sorry. Messed up horribly. Drawers open, bed-clothes yanked off. But she says nothing is missing. And nothing was torn or broken, for all the mess it was. And then the deodorant trick on Beth."

"My lab man says he's pretty sure it's something you can get in fishing and hunting stores. Something you either attract animals with or scare them off, I don't remember which he said," Mel murmured.

"What do you think?" Jane asked.

He smiled at her. Dazzlingly, she thought. "About what? Practical jokes in general? They're dumb and these aren't even particularly elaborate or funny. Not like slipping a horsehair into someone's cigarette."

"You think *that's* funny? The male mind never ceases to amaze me. No, I mean what do you think about these jokes?"

"I don't know. I'm just taking the report. What do you think, Jane? You've gotten to know these women. Who do you think's doing it?"

"I have no idea. It obviously wasn't Lila, though. Some of the jokes didn't happen until after she was dead."

Mel went down the list, ticking off names. "Victims of the tricks were Pooky, Avalon, Beth, Mimi, Kathy, Avalon, Pooky, Beth, Crispy, Pooky, Avalon, Beth. Seems fairly evenly distributed. Do you really call these women by these silly names? I mean, to their faces?"

Jane ignored the question. "Mimi and Kathy had the least done. Just the alarm clocks."

"Could either one of them be doing the tricks and just included herself to avoid suspicion?"

"In theory. I can't imagine Mimi doing tacky, vulgar things, though. Certainly not the underwear trick. And she was really angry when the antique disappeared. She's the one who bullied everybody into forming search parties to look for it. Besides, she's just too nice to do stupid, nasty things."

Mel cast her a questioning, if not downright doubtful, glance. Jane started to object to his suspicion of her judgment, but caught herself. Actually, what did she know about Mimi? That she seemed very pleasant, open, and honest. But then, she'd also been told by at least two of the others what a wonderful actress Mimi was. Maybe it was all an act, carefully planned and rehearsed.

"What about Kathy? Is it her kind of thing?"

"I don't think so. She's vulgar, but has no sense of humor at all, not even a bad one that would think up practical jokes. And if she were to play jokes, they'd have a point. Some kind of ecological or antinuclear reference. She's terribly intense and certainly smart enough to plan better, more politically pointed tricks if she wanted to."

"Okay, let's examine this another way. What the point was. Trading the purse contents—"

"Sheer nuisance value," Jane said. "Maybe also to embarrass one or both of them by pointing out to someone else just what was in her purse. But neither of them seemed to have anything they shouldn't."

"The alarm clocks," Mel went on.

"Nuisance again. Or maybe, at a big stretch, to make sure somebody was awake all night? I don't know."

"That was the night of the murder."

"Yes, but you said she was already dead by midnight, and the clocks didn't start going off until around two in the morning."

"The underwear trick?" Mel said.

"Nuisance first. Crispy didn't know it was going to be returned and had to go buy more—remind me to tell you something else about that trip to the store. The return of her lingerie was clearly meant to embarrass her and it did. She was angry and humiliated."

"The antique?" Mel asked, then answered himself. "That might have been a genuine theft and the person had to hide it someplace until she could retrieve it and get it out of the house."

"I don't think so. It was 'hidden' in an empty wastebasket in the utility room. Just sitting there in the bottom, all by itself. If someone really meant to conceal it, it would have been easy to cover it up." A little breeze had sprung up and Jane pulled her sweater closer, shivering. She pulled the collar up and sniffed it. "Either the smell is going away or I'm getting used to it."

"I think it's blowing away. I can't smell it either anymore. I'll let you go inside in just a minute, Jane. You're sure nothing's missing from Avalon's room?"

"She says not. It's not like it was her home. It might take you forever at home to discern that something's missing. But when you're traveling, you only have a limited number of your belongings with you. It's fairly simple to take inventory."

"Then the deodorant stunt. What on earth was the point of that?" Mel asked.

"I suppose to cause Beth embarrassment. Again, it worked very well. She's a very reserved, dignified person and there she was, running around in the hallway, screaming and gagging, dressed only in a towel. As practical jokes go, that one was magnificent. Maybe it was the grand finale. I hope so."

Mel tapped his pen on the steering wheel absently. Jane wondered once again who'd given him such a nice writing implement. "Let's turn it one more direction," he said. "Let's look at the geography. Three of the tricks required off-site preparation."

"What do you mean?"

"The nasty underwear had to be purchased someplace and brought along. So did the alarm clocks and the smelly stuff for the deodorant. All small and easily brought along. But while they took advance planning, they could have been used on anybody. Nothing was specific to any individual."

"Yes?" It was interesting to see how his mind worked, examining the "evidence" from different viewpoints. Interesting, but not fruitful, as far as she could tell.

"The purse switch was purely on-site," he went on. "And again, could have been any two people, as it didn't reveal anything pertinent to either of them. The ransacking of Avalon's room, too, could have been anybody. It accomplished nothing, except to make work for you, and probably frighten the victim a bit."

"Uh-huh."

"But the theft of the antique stands apart. That couldn't have been just anybody."

"But it could. Everyone must have had something valuable along. Jewelry or credit cards or something."

Mel nodded. "True, I suppose. Had she mentioned this pen set or whatever it was? Before it was taken, I mean."

"Not to me. But maybe to somebody else."

"And I suppose it's already been mauled around by practically everybody?"

"Fingerprints, you mean? Yes, we passed it around admiring it after it was found. Sorry."

He waved this away. "Did these women know who else was coming to stay here?"

"I don't think so, unless some of them were in touch with each other. Shelley didn't even know until last week who was coming and she didn't send out a list or anything."

"Do they seem to know each other? Presently?"

"I don't think so. Beth said something about having a friend in common with Kathy who kept her up on Kathy's life a bit. Avalon and Pooky might correspond. They seem to be slightly better acquainted, or maybe they just hit it off better since they got here. Of course, most of them knew about Beth's prestige. No, on the whole, I don't think they're in touch with each other. That first day, as they were arriving, they were all catching up like mad—where did you end up going to college? Are you married? Have you got children? Those kinds of questions. Now, Lila was a different matter—"

"How's that?"

"She must have researched some of them before she came. At least she did Kathy."

"Remind me who Kathy is. The farm wife in the overalls?"

"Sort of. Wait till you see her today. She's abandoned her act."

"Act?"

Jane explained about Kathy's pretense of being poor and idealistic and Jane's own subsequent discovery of the truth of the matter.

"And she said Lila knew and was trying to blackmail her?"

"Trying, but not getting anywhere. Kathy's whole problem is that she's come to care more for her money than her image. She'd have faced 'unveiling' rather than give Lila a penny."

"Maybe. . . ." Mel mused. "What about the others? Did she try it with anyone else?"

"I think she had something on Pooky, but that's just pure guess. I asked Pooky outright and she denied it, but got very upset. Oh, I'd forgotten—there was something said the first night about Pooky having been held back a grade. Apparently that's very embarrassing to her."

"And the rest of them didn't know this?"

"I don't know. But it doesn't seem exactly blackmail material. Lila also dropped some not very subtle hints the first evening about Avalon and drugs. I think she was leading up to claiming Avalon had tried drugs in high school. Not exactly a revelation to ruin a life, I'd think. And she made some crack about Beth's life being placed under scrutiny if she was appointed to the Supreme Court. It sounded like a shot in the dark and didn't seem to bother Beth at all. Oh, and she tried to suggest that Mimi's husband was somehow politically questionable."

"How'd Mimi react?"

"Bored to death."

"What about Crispy? Did she go after her?"

"Not that I know of. Oh, yes. Lila made some rather cruel little digs about how enamored of Dead Ted Crispy had once been."

"Dead Ted?" Mel asked.

"Ted lived in this house when they were in high school. He committed suicide in the carriage house. It seems like they all had crushes on him back then. Mel, you haven't said how Lila was killed."

"Knocked out with a paint can, then smothered," he said calmly.

"Fingerprints?"

He shook his head. "The wire handle on the can had been wiped clean. A hell of a weapon, actually. You could hold the thing by the handle and get a good swing going in a dark place before the victim even saw it coming. And rags don't take fingerprints at all well."

"Come on, Mel. Tell me more of what *you* know."

"Very little yet. We better get inside. You're shivering and I've got to take Edgar's official statement."

"Mel, what about the practical jokes? What have they got to do with the murder? Are they just meant as a distraction? Or spite? Or what?"

"Hell if I know," he said. "Yet."

## 15

Jane let Mel go ahead and stood in the driveway a moment, still puzzling over what they'd talked about. It took a crazy to kill somebody. That was obvious. It also took something of a crazy to keep pulling these stupid jokes. It had to be the same person, unless one assumed that two of them were completely around the bend. That seemed impossible odds. Two out of seven. Two out of six, really. Lila couldn't have been either the murderer or the Joker.

*Lila!*

Jane remembered the notebook again. She'd meant to tell Mel a moment ago, but hadn't wanted to get sidetracked.

She hurried inside, but he was in the library with Edgar. Astonishingly, Mimi and Pooky were hunched in front of the television set, each with a Nintendo controller in her hand. They were competing loudly with each other in a shoot-'em-up game. "I got you! I got you!" Pooky crowed.

"I've got two lives left and three bottles of magic potion. I'll get you yet!" Mimi said, sitting farther forward and executing a complex maneuver that involved both hands and a lot of body English.

"Could you pause the game?" Jane asked. When they had, she said, "I'm going back to work. When Detective VanDyne's through, would you keep him here and let me know?" She started to say that there was something important she'd forgotten to tell him, then thought better of it. "I need to talk to him about some plans we made for next week."

"Next week? You're dating him?" Pooky asked. "Wow! He's really good-looking! Oh, so that's why you've been talking to him so much! It's nothing to do with us; it's that he's your boyfriend."

Jane realized she was blushing and stammering. "I've got to finish up the rooms," she said.

"I'll help," Pooky said.

"No, you're having fun. I'm almost done anyway." Jane made a break for it before Pooky could argue.

Beth was in her room, sitting in the grandmother chair by the window, reading through a stack of paperwork. There was a hint of the earlier horrible smell, but whether it came from Beth herself or just lingered in the room was impossible to say.

"No rest for the wicked?" Jane asked, gesturing toward the pile of work Beth was sorting through.

"More like no rest for the perpetually understaffed and underfunded."

"Are you all right now?"

Beth smiled and Jane could see for a moment what a very pretty girl she must have been. "I'm fine, thanks. I made a real fool of myself this morning. I'm so embarrassed. I normally don't overreact that way."

"Anybody would have. That was a horrible thing to do to you. Do you have any idea who—?"

"Absolutely none in the world," Beth said.

Jane had suspected that Beth would be too discreet to make guesses or get involved in gossip of any sort, but was disappointed to find that she'd been right.

"Do you know what it was? The smell?" Beth asked. Her voice was actually a bit trembly.

THE CLASS MENAGERIE 129

"Some kind of fish bait smell, I think. Harmless."

"Harmless . . ." Beth mused. "I didn't know . . ."

"Didn't know what?"

"That anybody disliked me that much." A definite crack in the last word.

"You shouldn't get your feelings hurt," Jane assured her. "I'm sure it wasn't personal any more than any of the other tricks. Maybe you're the only one who had that roll-on kind of deodorant along that the liquid could be added to. I'm sure that's it."

Beth smiled. "You're a nice person to say that. I hope you're right." Then she sniffed slightly, sat up straighter, and started sorting her papers. Obviously she wasn't accustomed to talking about her feelings to anyone and it made her very uncomfortable.

"Will I disturb you if I tidy up a little?" Jane asked. The room obviously couldn't be tidier, but she was supposed to change the sheets and towels.

"Not in the least. I still can't get over how generous it is of you to help Shelley. She's fortunate to have such a good friend." Unlike Pooky, it didn't occur to Beth to help out.

"I'm fortunate, too. I've had some bad times I wouldn't have gotten through without Shelley."

"Oh? I'm sorry to hear that."

There was invitation in her tone, but Jane didn't accept it. Jane knew how to encourage people to talk and recognized when the ploy was being used on her. "It's such a pity about Lila, isn't it?" She started stripping the bed.

"Nobody should come to a violent end," Beth said tactfully.

"What was she like as a girl? With the rest of you, I think I can guess what you must have been like, but not with her." Jane was determined to prod information or genuine opinion out of Beth, just for the challenge of the thing. Her brief confession of having her feelings hurt proved it could be done.

"Lila as a girl. . . ." Beth said, "Smart, certainly. A bit snobbish, but she did come from a very old, respected family. I believe she was ambitious, but without any specific focus of ambition, if you know what I mean."

"I think so. But most of us are like that. You're an exception."

"Me?"

"The others say you knew you wanted to be a lawyer even in high school." Jane shook out a fresh sheet and started making the bed.

"I suppose that's true. It's all so long ago—another life, almost. Another person."

"You feel you've changed so much?" Jane asked, surprised. From what the others had said, Beth seemed to have changed the least.

"Of course! Everybody does. Why, look at yourself. Try to remember how you felt about yourself, your parents, and your friends when you were eighteen. You probably don't feel the same way about any of them anymore."

"That's true. But I'm inclined to think people stay the same more than they change."

"Basic character traits, you mean? Maybe. And some, like Kathy, try desperately to stay the same."

Jane felt dizzy from the circular conversation. Beth wasn't going to let down her guard again. It probably only happened every ten years or so. Maybe shock tactics—

"It must be very difficult for you, staying here where Ted died."

There was a shocked, offended silence. Then surprisingly, Beth answered. "Not as much as I thought it would be. Teenage suicide can be devastating to everybody involved. It was horrible at the time, but as I got older, I realized it really had nothing to do with me. Suicide is always the sole responsibility of the person who commits it. It's characteristic of human nature that we wish to blame others for our problems, but in the end, our problems, or at least the way we deal with them, are our own. Even when they're very severe. Why in this case I'm studying—well, never mind. I didn't mean to get philosophical," she added with a laugh. "I'd better get out of your way."

And before Jane could say anything else, Beth had picked up her papers and left the room. *Don't be disappointed,* Jane told herself. *She didn't get where she is by gossiping with the hired help.*

"A notèbook? Belonging to the victim?" Mel asked. "Why in the world didn't you tell me about this sooner!" He was really angry.

"I kept meaning to and forgetting."

"You say she left it in your car?"

"Yes, Crispy had one just like it, and wanted to see what was in Lila's book, so she traded them somehow and got Lila's out of my car later."

"What was in it?"

"I have no idea. You'll have to ask Crispy."

Crispy was duly summoned. She looked smashing in a pink workout suit and understated pearl earrings. *That's a sweat suit that'll never get sweated on,* Jane thought.

"The notebook? Dull as dishwater," she said, not the least abashed at not having turned it over to the police. "Some numbers in a sort of chart that looked like she'd been pricing car insurance. A recipe for hummus. Some grocery coupons. The address for a jeweler in New York. Let's see—some airline times. Her flight, I believe. Nothing useful."

"Maybe you'd like to let me judge that for myself," Mel said stiffly.

"I'd be delighted to, but I can't. It disappeared."

"What!"

"I put it in with the lingerie I brought back. I left the bag on my bed to put things away later. And when I came back to my room, it was gone. Not the clothing. Just the notebook."

"Why didn't you say anything?" Jane asked, angry now too.

"I just forgot. Believe me, the notes in it were useless. Just the sort of stuff you'd jot down on the back of grocery lists and stick in your purse."

"If it turns up, you *will* turn it over to us," Mel said.

Crispy bounced to her feet. "Naturally."

Mel was drumming his fingers on the library table. "Jane, if you'd even told me this yesterday, I could have searched the house for it and probably found it. Nobody had gotten away. But today, they're scattered to the four winds."

That was true. It was a gorgeous day and even the most sedentary had gone for walks. Avalon and Pooky had breakfast dates with friends in town. The notebook could be miles away by now.

But at the same time, investigating this murder was Mel's job. His only job, while Jane's jobs had included taking care of her three children, cleaning up and helping with cooking at the bed and breakfast, trying to sneak time to write a few pages of her novel, and attending Back-to-School night. Plus, although it was not an assigned job, she had been on the spot for most of the jokes. Her brain was completely overloaded. But, in the interests of her relationship with Mel, she didn't say any of this. Instead, she just said, "I'm really sorry."

She'd hoped to ask him what he and the police department had found out about the women, but this wasn't the time. Besides, he was pretty good at being discreet himself. She knew what he'd say: "Jane, if a person doesn't have any criminal record, they hardly exist as far as we're concerned. I *can* dig up everything on a person's life, but not until I have them identified as a strong suspect." They'd had this conversation once before.

So she let him go, still angry, and went to help Edgar with lunch preparations. "We're almost done," Edgar said. "Only a light supper tonight; they're going to a cocktail party at the community center." He shuddered at the thought of what kind of foodstuffs would be served at the community center. "So for lunch we'll have baked sole, a nice Welsh rarebit, and a Boston lettuce salad with a lime/yogurt dressing. All fairly light and feminine. Then tonight, I thought chili and sandwiches. That's macho. Lots of celery and crackers. Cheeses and onions on the side."

"I'd reconsider the beans," Jane said.

Edgar laughed. "I'll go easy on the beans. Is Shelley ever coming back?"

"Not if she's smart," Jane replied.

They'd just started cleaning up lunch when the phone rang and Edgar handed it to Jane.

"Oh, Mom!" Katie wailed.

"What's wrong!"

"I forgot my gym shoes!"

Jane let out her breath, relieved. "I'll run home and get them. You be watching for me at the front door."

"Run along," Edgar said. "I can finish this up. And I don't need you back for dinner. I can manage it fine by myself."

Jane made a pitiful, insincere offer to come back anyway, but Edgar brushed it off and she took her chance to escape.

Katie bounded out to the car when Jane arrived at the junior high. "Guess what, Mom! Jenny and I have *dates* tonight!"

"No, you don't."

"Now, Mom, just listen for a minute. Jenny's dad is driving and it's okay with Jenny's mom."

This surprised Jane. Jenny's mother was as determined as Jane that the girls wouldn't date until they were thirty-five if she could manage it. "Jenny's mother agreed to this?"

"Yes, she says it's okay. Just talk to her, Mom. It's this really neat guy and, Mom, you have to face the fact that I'm *not* a child anymore."

It was tempting to point out that Katie was the living definition of a child, but Jane just said, "I'll talk to Jenny's mother. Do not take this as agreement."

But she had; she went tearing off like a happy gazelle. Jane glanced around, preparing to pull out, and noticed Shelley's car. And a second later, Shelley coming out of the school. Jane waved and went to meet her. "What are you doing here?"

"Some idiot decided this was a perfect day to annoy me about the children's vaccinations. I had to take a record to the office."

"You don't look very rested," Jane said.

"Rested! I'm the top contender for PMS Poster Girl! By the way, you don't need to go with me to that damned thing at the community center tonight."

"Geez, Shelley, I hadn't planned to. You seem to have come out of your shell."

"Shell? If I had a shell left, I'd use it to brain somebody with."

"There, there," Jane soothed. "As they say in the delivery room: It's almost over."

"With just the worst to come," Shelley said with a laugh.

## 16

"Hazel, have you lost your mind?" Jane was saying a few minutes later to Jenny's mother.

"Jane, where have you been? I've been trying to get you for two days. No, this is great. Wait till you hear. Come in."

"Can't," Jane said.

They settled on the little wrought iron bench by the front door. "All right, here's the deal. These little boys asked them out to a movie. It's one of those dreadful male things. Two hours of driving around in fast cars and shooting and gallons of testosterone sloshing everywhere. Howard wants to see it too—I'll never understand men—so he agreed to take the four of them. Don't you see—?"

Jane was smiling. "The girls will hate the movie, hate the boys, hate having a parent along and, with any luck, will hate the idea of ever having another date."

"Right! I knew you'd appreciate the plan!"

"I do. But it's still the thin edge of the wedge—"

"Jane, they don't have nunneries anymore that you pop daughters into."

"More's the pity. Okay. I'll go along with it. But if this doesn't work, you'll have to adopt Katie."

"I'd be glad to. We could just trade. I'm so pleased that the girls settled their differences. Jenny was ruining life as we knew it. Her brother and father were both

threatening to run away from home. And I was helping them pack. You're sure you can't come in for
a bit?"

"No, I've got to run."

Jane made her next stop the mall and headed for the
Foundations section of the anchor department store. A
towering, substantial platinum blond was waiting on
two elderly ladies, ringing up their purchases. "I think
you'll enjoy these, ladies, and if there's any problem,
just bring them back. Bye, now," she said, watching
after them and waving sweetly as they departed.

"If they bring those goddamned corsets back, I'll
choke their scrawny necks," she added to Jane. "So,
how's life treating you, Janie? You still dating that
hunky cop?"

"More or less. Listen, before another customer grabs
you, Suzie, were you here yesterday around noon?"

"Eternally. I'm part of the decor these days. There
are people who claim I was just standing here one day
in the middle of a field and they built the shopping
center around me."

"Do you remember an out-of-town customer, late
thirties, very stylish, bought a whole bag full of stuff?"

"A very expensive bag. I'll say. Friend of yours?"

"No, of Shelley's. I just gave her a lift."

"She said someone had stolen her underwear as a
joke. Strange kind of joke, if you ask me," Suzie said.
"Oops, just a sec. Got to flog some boob baskets."

Jane waited until Suzie was through showing indus-
trial strength underwear to another customer, then
sidled back up to her. "Here's the question, Suzie.
Did you notice if the woman put something else in
the bag?"

"Let me think." Suzie closed her eyes, concentrating. "Oh, yeah. She had this red notebook she kept

farting around with. Reading while I was ringing stuff up. Trying to shove in her purse, but it didn't fit. I think she tossed it in with the undies. Yeah, I'm sure she did. Why in the world do you care?"

"I don't know. I just wondered. You didn't happen to see what was written in it, did you?"

"Jane, do I look like I've got time or reason to care? Sorry, but I gotta get back to work. Give that VanDyne one for me."

"One what?"

"Whatever you're giving him," she said with a lewd wink.

*So Crispy was telling the truth about putting Lila's notebook in the shopping bag,* Jane thought as she went back to her car. Did it follow that the rest of the story was true? That she'd put the shopping bag on her bed, gone away, and returned to find the book gone? And what about her story about its containing only boring notes? Would Lila have been so frantic to get it back if that were the case?

Then Jane remembered the last time she'd priced car insurance. If she'd lost her notes and had to go through the whole confusing mess again, she'd have been frantic, too.

Preparing for Katie's date was like preparing for Desert Storm. The first requirement was a shopping blitz after school that cost the earth and left Jane hurriedly turning up a hem on a totally inappropriate dress at the last minute. She and Katie got into a slanging match over false eyelashes, which Katie lost, and about perfume, which Katie won.

"Mom! The kitchen's a mess!" Katie screamed at a quarter of seven. "What if they come in to get me?"

"Let me point out that I didn't make the mess," Jane said, exhausted and snappish. "And they won't come in because we will be standing at the door waiting when they drive up."

"We? *We!* Mom, you wouldn't—"

"I am meeting your date. Final."

Jenny was as dolled up as Katie, and in spite of her irritation, Jane got a lump in her throat looking at the two girls. They looked so cute and happy. The boys were already deep into an anticipatory discussion of the movie, making revving noises at each other. Jenny's dad was sitting behind the steering wheel, grinning. "We're going to the movie and then to Baskin-Robbins. I'll have her back by about ten," he said to Jane.

"Mom, can I go to Elliot's house and sleep over? He's got a new game and his mom said she'd take us for pizza," Todd said as she came back to the house.

"I guess so. Where have you been?"

"Hiding in the basement," Todd admitted. "All that girl stuff, ickkkk!"

Mike was asleep on the sofa. Jane turned off the television and he came awake as if he'd been nudged with a cattle prod. "What are you doing tonight?" Jane asked.

He rubbed his eyes furiously. "Nothing. Gotta study. Geez, Mom, I'm sick of school and I'm having to bust my buns this year just so I can go to school for another four years."

She sat down on the sofa and leaned against him. Willard, afraid somebody other than him was going to get petted, crawled up with them and tried to spread himself over both their laps. "It's the pits, isn't it?" she said sympathetically. "Want carryout Chinese for dinner?"

"Sounds good. You order while I take a shower and I'll pick it up. Get off me, Willard-Billard!"

The dog followed him upstairs.

Jane waited until the shower stopped running before ordering. As Mike backed out of the driveway, she stood watching and thinking. That was something else she was going to have to deal with soon. A car for Mike. Her wealthy mother-in-law Thelma kept offering—threatening—to buy him one. But it would be of her choosing and Mike was terrified of what she might get. "Mom, it'll be some awful old-lady car! Worse yet, she'd get herself something new and give me that big gray battleship she drives. I'd never live it down," he'd wailed when he heard of the offer. Jane didn't like the idea of being beholden to Thelma because Thelma was the sort who made sure you never forgot you were beholden.

Jane had to have more money. Her late husband's life insurance had all gone into trust funds for the kids—they had more assets than she did and she didn't have to worry about money for college. But she did have to get by day to day on part of Steve's share of the family pharmacy chain's profits. His share was equal to his mother's and brother's even though he wasn't alive and working there anymore, but Jane doggedly put half of it back into the trust funds. It really was the kids' money more than hers. The worst thing about that pharmacy money was that she had to accept it by hand from Thelma every month, who bestowed it grudgingly, like a gift that was far too good for the recipient.

That was part of the reason she was working—fitfully—on her book. Not that she really dreamed of ever making any money on it. Well, she did dream of it, but didn't take the dreams seriously. She'd also been checking books out of the library lately about real estate. Everybody told her the market was not booming at the moment, but if it got better, being a realtor might not be a bad choice. She could get out and meet people, which didn't happen when she was in her basement working on the novel. And it offered some independence. She'd love to say to Thelma, "Check? Oh, that check! I'd forgotten." She'd laugh merrily and stuff it in her purse without looking at the amount.

She was still engaged in this happy fantasy when Mike came back with the food. They ate off the coffee table in the living room, Mike channel-surfing the whole time with the remote control. After Jane cleaned up dinner, she got a jigsaw puzzle out and dumped it on the coffee table. "Got time to help me sort out the edges?" she asked.

"Sure. Calculus can wait." Mike said.

Within minutes Meow was daintily picking her way through the puzzle, sniffing pieces. "I forgot," Jane said. "This is the one the cats like."

"I think Todd put a tuna fish sandwich down on it once. Right on the barn. They always go for the red pieces."

They sorted edges, rescued red pieces from the cats, and watched television for a while. "How come you aren't over at what's-it tonight?" Mike asked, fitting two long sections together.

"The reunion? Shelley let me off duty."

"I don't get it. Reunions," Mike said. "Once I'm through with high school, I'm gonna be through. There's nobody I'll want to see again."

"Not even Scott?"

"Oh, I'll never get rid of Scott," Mike said with a laugh. "But we aren't friends 'cause we go to school together. We're just friends."

"But you wouldn't really go to a reunion?"

"What's the point? Those are the people who knew you when you were a dumb kid. I want to really be somebody, without a bunch of people reminding me how I accidentally dumped a lemonade all over my first date, or having a good laugh about putting the mouse in my tuba and I threw up when I discovered I'd been blowing the thing around in there. Or how I failed my driver's test because I ran a red light—"

"Mike! You told me you failed the written part!"

"I lied, Mom. It was for your own good," he added with a grin. "But, geez, who wants to be reminded of that stuff?"

"I don't understand reunions either," Jane admitted. "But then, I didn't go to one school for long enough to even remember my classmates. I think, though, that some people like them for just the reason you said. They grew up and got to be 'somebody' and they come so that everybody else will know it. And the ones who didn't become somebodies probably come so they can pretend that they are."

"Waste of time," Mike pronounced judgment. "I figure this is the worst time of my life. At least this week is. It's gotta get better and I don't want to relive this. Todd said he heard one of those women died. I told him he was full of it."

"One of them did," Jane said.

"What was it? Heart attack?"

"I don't know, exactly," Jane said. She didn't want to tell him it was murder because he'd worry about her needlessly. Whatever the reason, it had nothing to do with her, so she was in no danger. Besides, the reunion was nearly over. A picnic tomorrow afternoon, a dinner dance at the country club, and Sunday morning they'd all go home and, with any luck at all, Jane would never see any of them again.

Mike burrowed back into the sofa with his books and Jane continued working on the puzzle, plucking a green piece off Willard's nose as he went by. She blotted it on a napkin and put it in place.

At about nine-thirty, the doorbell rang. "Shelley, what are you doing here?"

"Hiding?"

"Come in." The phone rang as she was walking past it. She answered it, listened, and said, "Mike? It's for you." She covered the phone and mouthed, "It's a girl."

She waited until he'd picked up on the upstairs extension, then gently hung up. "I wonder what would happen if I said to one of them, 'Look here, you little hussy! Leave my son alone!' "

"Not much. Paul's mother's still saying that to me."

Jane laughed. "Would it help if I told you that you looked smashing?"

"Not much, but you can try. Jane, we need to talk—"

## 17

"So you let her go on a date?" Shelley asked a few minutes later when she'd taken off her shoes and knocked back half a glass of diet Coke.

"The date from Hell. Hazel and I are hoping."

"So she's made up with Jenny? What was their fight about?" Shelley was leaning back in her chair and had her eyes closed.

"Jealousy. The new girl. I think."

"Isn't it amazing the things kids can get worked up about?" Shelley said.

"Oh, I don't know that they're so bad. Neither of them put anything in the other's deodorant. Unlike some adults I know."

"Isn't it a nightmare?" Shelley said.

"Who do you think is playing the tricks? Not to mention killing Lila. . . ."

"You think it's the same person?" Shelley asked.

"I assume so. Unless you've got two nut cases."

"I think they're all nuts!"

"Do you really?"

Shelley sat up. "No, I really don't. That's what's so weird about this. They're all very distinct, some with strong personalities, but none of them seems like the kind to play stupid stunts, much less murder anybody. I still think it must have been someone from outside. It had to be, Jane!"

"Maybe—"

"Look, as obnoxious as she was to the Ewe Lambs, Lila didn't get that way overnight. She's had long years of practice making people miserable. And being made miserable. She could have had an enemy who followed her here and bumped her off where it could be blamed on someone else."

"That seems sort of baroque."

"Oh, I didn't tell you—Trey Moffat, he's our class president, said at the cocktail party tonight that he knew somebody who knew Lila. Interesting gossip. Apparently she married some no-neck bodybuilder and set him up in business as a private detective. She was assumed to be the brains of the outfit. Anyhow, he learned just enough about snooping to get some kind of goods on her, then divorced her. Trey wasn't sure what the compromising stuff was, but it must have been good. He cleaned her out. The bodybuilder. Not Trey."

"What do you mean?"

"The husband kept everything. The house, the agency, the bank accounts. That's why she was so hard up. The family money is gone, if there ever was much. I don't think there ever was a whole lot of money, just illustrious ancestors."

"You'll have to tell Mel that."

"I already did. He was at the cocktail party. Put a bit of a damper on things, in fact."

"I take it that you wouldn't be here if the party had been fun."

"Oh, it wasn't so bad. I was just sick of smiling and nodding. And I haven't had a real chance to talk to you for days."

"Has Constanza broken into your safe yet?"

Shelley giggled wickedly. "She made a big deal

of telling me how she'd spilled something and was
looking for a tablecloth and *just happened to notice*
that we'd gotten a safe. I tried to make her explain
why she was looking for a tablecloth in an upstairs
closet when there's a whole stack of them in the
laundry room. That made her squirm. That safe has
already paid for itself in satisfaction."

"Did she try to get the combination?"

"Repeatedly. She called Paul in Singapore with
a cock-and-bull story about having brought along a
valuable bracelet and she'd feel so much better if she
could put it away safely."

"And?"

"Paul told her he doesn't know the combination.
Which is true. I told her I'd lost the combination,
which isn't true, but said I'd take her straight down
to the bank and she could put her terribly valuable
bracelet in our safe deposit box. Then she decided
the bracelet wasn't so valuable after all and she'd just
keep on wearing it. Anyway—the party wasn't so bad.
Trey Moffat looks like the Pillsbury Doughboy. Has a
cute little wife and roly-poly baby along."

Jane had no interest in the class president. "Did you
pick up any other gossip?"

"Not much. The guy Pooky was bringing the pen set
to is a nerdy, single plastic surgeon. They seemed to
be hitting it off awfully well. Maybe there's a romance
in the air."

"I hope so. I've gotten to really like Pooky. I know
she's got the IQ of a kitchen appliance, but she's a
good-hearted person."

"Is she? I didn't really get a chance to talk to
her much. And when she did talk at the fund-raising
meeting, I wanted to smack her. Her suggestions were
so dumb. Good-hearted, as you say, but criminally

stupid. A telethon fashion show, for God's sake!"

"I never asked. . . . does she have children?"

Shelley thought a moment. "I think there was a child in one marriage. But it didn't belong to either of them. Avalon was talking about it in the car. The husband had married before, this was his stepchild and the wife died, then he married Pooky. They later divorced and the child went with him. Apparently it's a source of great grief to Pooky."

"Poor Pooky. Was everybody impressed with Crispy at the party?"

"Stunned senseless."

There was the sound of a key in the kitchen door, then Katie calling good-night before stomping into the living room. "Mom!—Oh, hi, Mrs. Nowack."

"Katie, did you have fun?" Shelley asked.

"Fun? Fun! What a couple of dweebs!"

Neither Jane nor Shelley, to their credit, cracked a smile.

"It was a horrible, dumb movie. All these stupid car crashes. And Johnny didn't even offer to share his popcorn with me. What mega-losers! And we went out for ice cream after and all they talked about was cars, cars, cars. Even Jenny's dad! Bo-o-o-ring! I've got to go call Jenny."

"You've just been with Jenny for three hours."

"But we couldn't really talk. 'Night, Mom."

Of unspoken accord, Jane and Shelley hadn't gotten into really serious discussion, knowing they were going to be interrupted shortly. When Katie had gone upstairs, Shelley leaned forward and said quietly, "So what has Mel told you?"

"Practically nothing. He's furious with me. About the notebook."

"What notebook?"

"What notebook! We *have* fallen behind if you don't know about the dreaded notebook." Jane explained to Shelley about Crispy's getting her hands on Lila's notebook, then subsequently having it stolen. "But you know how hectic things have been. I kept meaning to tell him, but other things happened. It wouldn't have mattered if I'd told him earlier anyway, because it disappeared within an hour of Crispy's finding it anyway."

"Do you think she's telling the truth? About it not having anything interesting in it? And about it being stolen?"

"About what was in it, yes, I think so. But about it being stolen, no. But I haven't any reason whatsoever for doubting her. It's just my instinct. I think she'd have held onto it and tried to read something into the notations."

"That would be my guess, too. That, or—"

"Or what?"

Shelley stood up and paced for a minute, curling her toes into the carpet as she walked. Willard heaved himself to his feet and walked alongside her, looking up expectantly. Shelley petted his head absently. "Look, Lila was trying to put the squeeze on people. Blackmail them out of money. Right?"

"It looks like it from what Kathy said."

"So whatever she knew about them might have been written in the notebook."

"She couldn't have remembered?"

"Not if she had specifics to toss at them. Like, maybe she had the exact amount of Kathy's holdings in some South African company or other, just to convince her that she knew what she was talking about. Blackmail isn't among my skills, but I'd think you'd have to have some concrete information to do it well."

"Okay, I'll buy that—"

"She might have made it look like innocent information, just in case she lost the book, as she did. Or in case someone else saw it. You'd hardly expect her to title the pages, What I'm Using for Extortion on Kathy. So Crispy might have genuinely thought it was boring stuff."

Jane thought for a minute. "Or, she thought it was boring stuff until she saw the part that pertained to her."

"Was Lila trying to blackmail her, too?"

"She's never said. She didn't try anything with you, did she?"

"I'm too boring to blackmail," Shelley said, "But she did give it a shot—I think. She made some crack about Paul and how she imagined with all those franchises, he had a lot of trouble with the income tax people. I said no, he had no trouble at all, which was an outright lie. Paul is constantly fighting them. Anyway, I didn't get it at the time, but later I realized she probably meant it as the groundwork for a threat. As in, Paul *will* have trouble with the IRS if you don't— whatever. Somehow, I can't imagine her having anything on Crispy that Crispy wouldn't be thrilled to talk about. She loves scandalizing people."

"No, her cracks at Crispy all seemed to have to do with Crispy's having such a hopeless crush on Ted."

"Ted! I'm sick of hearing of Ted. This has turned into the Ted Francisco Memorial Reunion."

"What about Ted? Do you think he committed suicide?"

"What a weird question. Of course he did. Unless you think you've seen him lately."

"No, I mean Crispy thinks it was an accident. That

he started up the car and went back for something,
fell over drunk, and died later."

"That's probably wishful thinking on her part,"
Shelley said, "but I suppose it could be true. Interesting—"

"What do you think? Was Ted the type to kill
himself?"

Shelley laughed. "Oh, Jane. Ted wouldn't have
known me if he'd fallen over me. I was not part of his
crowd. I didn't know him at all, except to adore from
afar. But since you ask, on the surface of it, it didn't
seem logical. Of course suicide never does. You don't
think Ted has something to do with this, do you?"

"Good Lord! I hope not! No, I was just curious.
Everybody keeps talking about him."

"Let's get back to the matter at hand," Shelley said
in her best Madame Chairwoman voice.

"Okay. Lila and blackmail. Most of the nasty things
she was saying seemed to have more to do with high
school than the present."

"What do you mean?"

"Well, she was hinting about Avalon doing drugs
in high school. Did she, by the way?"

"I have no idea. I wouldn't be surprised. What about
Pooky? Did she have anything on her?"

"I'm pretty sure she did, but Pooky's not admitting
it." Jane recounted her conversation with Pooky about
Lila's and Pooky's distress.

"What deep, dark secrets could high school girls
really have?" Shelley said. "Today they might, but
not back then."

"Well, drugs. Abortion, maybe. I don't know—a
drunk driving conviction?"

"That would have been juicy stuff then, but not
now. Most women our age would just say, 'Yes, isn't

it awful. I made a terrible mistake. Thank God it's in the past.' And that would be the end of it. We all did dumb things we'd cringe at being reminded of, but nothing we'd kill somebody for mentioning."

"What would somebody kill to protect?" Jane said.

They both thought long and hard for a moment, then Shelley said, "A child? Could somebody have a child Lila had some means of taking away? Let's see. Beth hasn't any children. Kathy's got a mob of them, but that's not what Lila was using on her. Avalon's got one of her own and the foster children. Crispy has none of her own, but half a dozen stepchildren from all those marriages."

"I think Mimi has two," Jane added. "She showed me a picture of two little girls. Pooky hasn't got any, you say. Speaking of children—" Jane turned her head toward the stairway, where they could hear sounds of an escalating battle upstairs. "I think my darlings, who both believe themselves to be independent adults, are squabbling over the phone."

She got up to go sort it out.

"We're going about this all wrong," Shelley said to her back.

"That much seems obvious," Jane tossed back. *"Michael! Katherine!"*

## 18

"I'm starving. Have you got anything to eat here?" Shelley asked when Jane came back from yelling at the kids. "Preferably something salty and crunchy with the highest fat content possible?"

"Crackers and cheese?"

"Doesn't sound greasy enough, but it would do."

Shelley slumped on a kitchen chair while Jane got out snacks. "How about some hot chocolate, just to run the calorie count up?" Jane asked.

"Sounds wonderful."

While Jane worked, Shelley said, "I don't believe in cholesterol. I think within ten years they'll change their trendy little medical minds and say they were wrong all along and human beings really need as many saturated fats as they can knock back. They're already changing their minds about eggs."

"Interesting theory."

"Jane, consider this: human beings are carnivores. The species developed in the jungle eating other creatures, finding eggs to steal, maybe eating the occasional plant, just for variety or out of desperation. I think red meat and eggs are the stuff of which humans are made."

Jane set down a tray and two cups of steaming cocoa. She'd even put little marshmallows in the cups. "In that case, I'll be ready with my cabinets full of

152

previously forbidden foods. Shelley, to get back to the subject at hand—this morning Mel was asking me about the practical jokes and he did something interesting that we ought to try."

"What's that?"

"He made a list of the jokes and then went through it over and over, looking at them each time in a different way. Like, were they harmful? Who was the victim? Could they have a meaning? Did they require advance preparation?"

"Uh-huh. And did it lead him to any conclusion?"

"Not that I know of. Not then. But it's an interesting way of looking at things."

"Okay . . . ?"

"So, let's do the same thing with the murder. We need to think about this in an organized, logical way."

"All right. Where do we start?" Shelley took an extremely unladylike bite of a cracker she'd slathered with a great deal of cheese.

"Well, how about this—if we agree that Lila was killed because she was blackmailing someone—"

"Do we know that?"

Jane thought for a minute. "No, actually we don't *know* it. It just seems extremely likely."

"Likely isn't certain."

"No, but why else would somebody kill her?"

"Oh, any number of reasons, starting with the fact that she was an all-round obnoxious bitch."

"Yes, but there are a lot of those in the world, and most of them are still alive and kicking."

"Unfortunately," Shelley said with a grin.

"Okay, we can come back later to reexamine our basic premise. But for now, let's pretend that we *know* Lila was killed because she was blackmailing someone."

"Okay by me. Lead on, Sherlock." Shelley took a careful sip of her cocoa and closed her eyes appreciatively for a moment. "You have a great skill with premixed foodstuffs, Jane."

"All right. Let's look at our list of suspects," Jane went on.

"Who's on the list?"

"The Ewe Lambs," Jane said uneasily.

"And who else?"

"I don't know. Shelley, you know perfectly well it has to be one of them."

"No, I don't and neither do you."

Jane knew when she was on thin ice. "You might be right. But since we don't know who the other suspects may be, let's just talk about the ones we do know."

Shelley nodded grudgingly.

"So, let's consider first who had the opportunity."

"Anybody, I'd say. It depends on when she was killed, doesn't it? I mean, she was out in the carriage house and found after everybody was locked in. But maybe she was killed before that. Before ten-thirty."

"Then it would have to have been between nine-thirty and ten-thirty. Right?"

"She and whoever it was couldn't have gone out the kitchen door between those times, could they?" Shelley asked.

"I don't think so. Somebody or other was in the kitchen all the time. But there are doors all over the house."

"I don't think this is getting us anywhere, Jane. It needn't have taken more than a few minutes to smack her with a paint can—isn't that what somebody said happened?—and smother her. And it's not messy like stabbing or something. The murderer wouldn't have had to sneak inside and wash blood off her clothes or anything like that. Just slip quietly back in the door she'd left by and pick up where she left off as if she'd just been to the bathroom or something."

"Hmmm—"

"By the way, Mel was back this afternoon questioning everybody again. Exact movements and times. I actually felt sort of sorry for him."

"Did he seem depressed when he got done?"

"Very. Understandably. Most of us, in our normal lives, could give a pretty good account of what we did and when. We're tied to household schedules or office schedules or whatever. But this was meant as a vacation. Everybody I know turns their mental clocks off when they're on a trip. I certainly do."

"Not only that, he's got a couple of hours of night to consider," Jane said. "When the only reasonable answer to 'where were you?' is 'in bed.' Even though it might not have been true of one of them."

"Jane, this method of yours doesn't seem to be doing us any more good than it did Mel."

"Then let's try looking at it another way. Who has the most to lose? From Lila's blackmail."

"Since we don't know what she was blackmailing each of them about—"

"No, assume for a moment that she had something truly horrendous on each of them. Who had the most to lose?"

"Everybody, I'd say. If she knew something really awful, awful enough to send them to prison, for example, it could be anyone."

"But I doubt that it was anything like that. The one we know about, Kathy and her secret wealth, was merely embarrassing. The rest were probably variations on that sort of thing. Unless you assume that somebody *did* have something really terrible in her background. Gave away national military secrets or robbed a bank or the like."

"Well, I'd say probably Beth, then. She's the one whose reputation is most important to her life. But I simply cannot imagine Beth ever doing anything that would even slightly endanger her reputation."

"But it's pretty widely assumed that old Ted killed himself because she broke up with him. That could be considered a blot," Jane said.

"As you say, 'widely assumed.' It's no secret. And as you yourself reported, some of them tend to believe— or want to believe—that it was just a drunken accident that had nothing to do with her."

"Yeah . . . well, maybe some legal decision that she ruled on, but had some involvement with the participants that she didn't admit?"

"Can you really imagine that? She's the most self-controlled person I've ever known. I think she stands outside herself constantly saying, 'Is there any way this could be misinterpreted and if so, I won't do it.' Especially with her career, which is her life."

"You're right. Well, what about Kathy then? Suppose there was more to it than just having a lot of money. Suppose she'd been doing inside trading?"

"I think you have to be a stockbroker to be guilty of inside trading."

"I just meant that as an example. Suppose she'd been doing some kind of hanky-panky with manipulating stocks. She's certainly bright enough."

Shelley got up and poured them each another cup of cocoa. "Okay, I'll buy that. But how would Lila know?"

Jane shrugged. "I've no idea. But Lila was pretty smart, too, and she had run a detective agency. What a bizarre job that was for somebody so prim and proper. Anyway, she knew where and how to look for information about people."

"What about the others then? Like Crispy? What would Crispy have to lose? Her life and many marriages are not only an open book, they're a book she forces on everybody who gets within shouting range."

"Bigamy?" Jane suggested.

Shelley shook her head. "They don't stone people or lock them up for that anymore. It's just a civil thing a bunch of expensive lawyers would sort out."

"What if she's not rich at all? Maybe she's dirt-poor and just putting on a show? The opposite of Kathy's act?"

"What good would it do you to blackmail a poor person?"

Jane laughed. "Good point. I'm better with imagination than logic."

"Let it loose on Pooky then," Shelley said. They'd finished the crackers and she was licking her finger and prodding bits of crumbs out of the package they'd been in.

"Pooky—okay, here goes. She won that gigantic lawsuit against the guy who wrecked her face, right? Suppose Lila knew that the guy actually hadn't done it wrong, but Pooky herself did something that made it go bad? Like they say you can't smoke after you have a face-lift or the scars won't heal right."

"I hardly think they mean you'll end up looking like Pooky if you take a drag."

Jane was getting impatient, but tried to hide it. "Shelley, it was just an example. What if—ah, what if she'd gone home with relatively harmless goop on her face and washed it off with something that caused a chemical reaction? If Lila knew that and threatened to tell, Pooky's suit might have been reversed and she'd have to give the money back."

"You picture Lila spying through her bathroom window at exactly the right moment."

"Shelley, you're not playing this game right. I don't know how she'd know, but suppose she did?"

"I'll give you a real weak maybe on that one. What about Mimi?"

"Oh, Mimi's easy. Immigration authorities. What if there'd been something fishy when her parents brought the whole family to this country? Lila might have known something that would cause all of them to be in danger of being shipped back to China. As happy as Mimi is with her heritage, I don't think she's champing at the bit to go back. And she's married to a Soong. There might be something political in that."

"Like being married to a Smith. I'll give you that this one's possible. Not likely, but possible. But again, why would Mimi kill her? Wouldn't she just traipse off to a lawyer and ask him to fix things?"

"Not if it weren't fixable. Who did we leave out?"

"Avalon."

"Drugs," Jane said quickly. "Lila seemed to be hinting that Avalon had experimented with drugs in high school. But what if she meant recently? What if she meant trafficking?"

Shelley burst into laughter. "All run through a crafts boutique in the Ozarks? Jane, I adore you!"

Jane tried to be miffed, but grinned in spite of herself. "Okay, but keep in mind that you're laughing because it's so unlikely. What better cover than the most unlikely one? Tell me that!"

"Yes, yes, but it's like trying to picture Noriega with overalls and a corncob pipe."

They were still laughing when they heard a light tap on the kitchen door. They looked at each other, slightly alarmed. The kitchen clock said quarter of eleven.

"Probably one of Mike's friends," Jane said.

She went to the door and pulled aside the curtain before opening it. "Mel? What are you doing here?"

"I hope it's not too late. I saw your lights were on."

"Come in. Shelley and I were just pigging out."

He looked a bit disappointed at the mention of Shelley, but said, "Hello, Mrs. Nowack."

They hadn't much liked each other from the time they'd met and it was Shelley who'd insisted on being *Mrs.* Nowack.

"Come in, Detective VanDyne," she said. "And tell us all you know."

It wasn't a request, it was an order.

## 19

Shelley must have seen Jane's back stiffen, because she quickly said, "If you don't mind telling us, that is. And I think maybe we should be Mel and Shelley to each other. For Jane's sake, if nothing else."

Mel glanced at Jane, who gave him a "don't you dare be sarcastic" look.

"I think that's a good idea, Shelley," he said politely.

Mel sat down at the kitchen table across from Shelley and they made excruciatingly courteous small talk while Jane searched frantically through her cabinets and refrigerator to find other snacks. Hoping they couldn't see what she was doing, she sliced a tiny spot of mold off the end of a nice rectangle of sharp cheddar cheese. She dumped some Wheat Thins that were so stale she could practically bend them onto a cookie sheet and popped it into the oven.

"Jane was telling me about discussing the practical jokes with you and the method you used of looking at them in different ways," Shelley said, sounding rather formal. "We were trying it out on the murder, but Jane's imagination ran amok and we ended up with Colombian drug kings in the hills of Arkansas."

"Oh?" he said, not laughing.

Shelley recounted the theories they'd been discussing. Jane thought Shelley was trying to give him, if not information, at least a facsimile of facts, in order to persuade him to share information in return. A hopeless cause. Mel would tell them exactly as much as he wanted to and no more.

"But we started with two assumptions that I question," Shelley finished up. "The first was that Lila was killed because she was blackmailing someone and the second was that it was one of the Ewe Lambs who did it." There was query in her tone.

"On the second point, I think you can assume that," he said to Shelley's obvious displeasure. "The lab people have crawled over the house and found evidence that someone put a rock in the opening of the utility room door to hold it open. The door must have struck the rock pretty hard and there's a clear match between the door and a decorative rock."

"But—"

He put up a hand to stop her. "The door was only installed a week earlier. Edgar and Gordon had no reason to ever prop it open before your people arrived. They had the key to it, remember. So it appears that somebody went out after lockup and needed to be sure she could get back in without being detected doing so."

"There isn't an alarm that would go off?" Jane asked.

"There will be when they've got the place ready to open officially, but since you needed the space before that, there were several things undone."

Jane rescued the crackers, which were beginning to smell a little singed.

"So that means she was killed between ten-thirty when Edgar locked up and twelve-thirty or whenever the boys saw her body," Shelley said in a defeated voice. "And it means that somebody staying *in* the bed and breakfast did it."

"Probably," Mel said.

"What do you mean, probably?" Shelley demanded. "I thought that was your whole point."

"No, you're leaping to conclusions. Probably the right ones, I'll admit. All that this *proves* is that somebody went outside after ten-thirty, somebody who came back, threw or kicked the rock back into the garden, and let the door close and lock. Now, Lila obviously went out, but she didn't come back. But somebody else, in theory, could have gone out to meet her, found her already dead, and come back in."

"—or gone out for some other reason entirely," Jane put in. "Maybe didn't even go to the carriage house."

Mel nodded. "—and couldn't afford to admit it the next morning. Although I can't see why anybody would need to sneak out for any other reason. We're not talking about kids with a curfew."

Jane set the tray of crackers and cheese down and sat next to Mel. "Are you telling us you think that's what happened? That somebody went out for another reason and found her?"

"No, I think it's extremely unlikely. But it *is* possible. I'm just pointing out that the physical evidence doesn't conclusively have to do with the murder."

*Putting us in our imaginative places,* Jane thought.

"What about our first premise, that Lila was killed because of her blackmail attempts?" Shelley asked.

"Well, that's a matter of endless interviews and intuition, not physical facts," Mel said.

"Of course it is, but what do you think?" Shelley insisted. She was coming close to asking what she really wanted to know, which was what additional information Mel had about the suspects.

"I think—personal opinion only—that it's extremely likely, in view of the fact that she attempted extortion on at least one of the women and hinted at secret information about others. But there are a lot of reasons for murder, some of them pretty loony."

"Loony—" Jane said. "Have any of them ever been hospitalized for any mental aberrations? I mean, what if it was just a crazy act with no motive?"

Mel treated this question with the minimum respect due it. "If that's the case, we'll eventually dig far enough to discover it."

"Eventually," Shelley said. "It's a shame they all live elsewhere. It will make it harder to pursue, won't it? What other motives have you looked at?"

"Inheritance is one of the first we consider," Mel said. "But it doesn't appear that she had very much to leave anyone; so far it's just a lot of bills, and if there's anything left, it's to go to a second cousin who's been in France for the whole month and hardly seemed to remember who Lila was."

"What about revenge?" Jane asked, nibbling one of the crackers. It really did have a slightly charred taste. "What if she'd done something really nasty to one of the Ewe Lambs years ago and this was just the first time the murderer had gotten close enough to her to do her in?"

She could see from Mel's expression that he hadn't considered this, but was rejecting it as fast as he thought about it. "But if you wanted to kill her and get away with it, you'd make sure you *weren't* known to be anywhere near," he said.

Shelley said, "Listen, this is really dumb and I know it, so don't jump all over me, but—I was reading a book last week about a man who killed himself, but set it up to look like his wife had done it to revenge himself on her for something. That's not remotely possible, is it? Lila was certainly nasty enough to want to see somebody else suffer along with her. And she was apparently at a low point in her life if she was reduced to committing extortion. And remember, the extortion attempts weren't going well for her. If this reunion was her very last attempt to hang onto her life and it blew up in her face—? After all, she did die where Ted killed himself so long ago. In the carriage house."

Jane looked uneasily at Mel, afraid he was going to dismiss Shelley's theory in terms that would put them back to *Mrs. Nowack* and *Detective VanDyne* with her smoothing feathers in the middle.

But he came through like a champ.

"It's possible and the psychology might account for a lot," he said, "but the physical evidence refutes it. She might have struck herself in the temple with the paint can hard enough to inflict a severe wound, but then she'd have had to remain conscious to wipe the fingerprints off the can, as somebody did. And then smother herself. That one's pretty hard to do. Not impossible, of course. She could have forced her own face into the rags, but then she'd have been facedown, not faceup as she was found."

Shelley smiled at him. It was the first time Jane could remember Shelley's actually smiling sincerely at Mel. "Thanks," she said. "Just to be positive— I don't suppose the boys who discovered her could have turned her over?"

"They were so traumatized by merely seeing her, I don't think you could have gotten them to touch her if you'd put guns to their heads."

They sat quietly for a moment; Shelley was gazing into her cocoa, now cold and getting a nasty skin. Jane munched another disgusting cracker.

"Aren't you going to ask me?" Mel finally said, breaking the silence.

"Ask you what?" Jane said.

"What I've learned about the Ewe Lambs—God, what a name! I can hardly stand to say it. It's like being forced to order something by a cute name in a restaurant."

"We didn't think you'd tell us," Shelley said.

Mel took a cracker, bit into it, and looked unpleasantly surprised.

"Oh, just spit it out in this napkin," Jane said.

He swallowed melodramatically and patted her thigh in a *very* friendly manner. "Ladies, you know I'm not supposed to share information with you, but in light of the fact that you were both at the bed and breakfast that night, and because you have occasionally provided me with some interesting information that helped in solving a case—"

"Helped!" Jane exclaimed. "We solved—"

He held up his hand again.

"You could be a crossing guard if you get tired of detecting," Jane said. "Okay, I'll shut up. Just tell us what you know."

"Understood that this is absolutely confidential?" he asked.

They both nodded.

"For now and forever?"

Jane laughed. "Cross our hearts and hope to die. Maybe there's a Ewe Lamb Oath we could take, too. Shelley? Like, I promise I'll never go ba-a-a-ack on my word—"

"I thought you'd gotten over that," Shelley said coldly.

"I thought I had, too. Must have just been a momentary relapse. So, we promise, Mel."

He said, "As I've told Jane before, my staff can only easily find out about people if they've had a bout with the law, either an arrest or a lawsuit—"

"And one of the Ewe Lambs has a record?"

"One has a record. And one has a lawsuit. Your Pooky."

"Oh, we know about that," Shelley said. "She sued the man who ruined her face and got a big settlement."

"That's not the suit I mean. It was a very nasty divorce proceeding that involved criminal charges. Deborah—"

"You mean Pooky?" Jane asked.

"Yes," Mel replied. "I just *can't* call a grown human being 'Pooky.' Deborah was married to a man who had adopted his previous wife's son. When Deborah married him, she also adopted the child. Reading between the lines, it appears that when she lost her looks, her husband lost interest in her, but became very interested in her money from the settlement. They divorced and it went well enough until it came to custody of the child. Since the boy wasn't genetically related to either of them, it seemed likely that Deborah would get custody. But at the last moment, her soon-to-be-ex-husband filed charges against her, claiming she'd sexually abused the boy."

"No!" Jane said, horrified. "That's impossible!"

"The judge agreed. It seems to have been a pretty blatant last-ditch effort to get at her money through the boy. The husband was trying to claim alimony, child support, and psychological damages on behalf of the child."

"What a jerk!" Shelley said. "Poor old Pooky! As if life hadn't treated her badly enough."

"As I say, the judge agreed. But he decided that the

boy should go with the adoptive father, with whom he'd lived before the marriage anyway. The husband didn't get a penny. But he did get the child."

"Yes!" Jane said suddenly. "I remember now! Lila said something about Pooky understanding the psychology of boys. I thought it was a dig about Pooky as she was in high school, implying that she slept around, but I'll bet that's what she meant. And the accusation still stands in the legal record," Jane said. "Available to anyone who knows how and where to look."

"Like Lila," Shelley said. "Poor Pooky. . . ."

## 20

Mike came downstairs, said hello to Shelley and Mel, got a carton of orange juice, and went back upstairs. When he was out of earshot, Shelley spoke to Mel again. "You mentioned somebody having a record?"

He nodded. "Avalon—and Jane wasn't so far off."

"Drug kings in the Ozarks?"

"Not drug kings, but there was definitely a handoff of some kind that went on at their house. The drug squad had been following a dealer. Avalon and her husband claimed to have no knowledge of what was going on and there wasn't any proof that they were directly involved except to allow the parties into their home. Still, the foster children were all taken out of their keeping for a year. They were charged, but the charges were later dropped for lack of evidence. They got the kids back eventually. Some kids. I don't know if it was the same ones."

"So Lila could have had knowledge of this, through the legal records," Jane said.

"But why would she go after Avalon?" Shelley asked. "Supporting all those kids, she can't have much money. And she runs a little craft store and lives off in the hills someplace. . . ."

"There are mansions in those hills these days," Mel said. "And if Lila believed that Avalon and her husband were still involved in drug traffic, she could have assumed they had lots and lots of money. As they might. Has she ever talked about her house? How she lives?"

Jane and Shelley exchanged questioning looks. "Not around me," Shelley said.

"Me neither," Jane added. "The only time I heard her mention her home was something about having to build a ramp to the porch to accommodate a wheelchair. But she didn't indicate anything about the size of the house."

"You've found nothing on Crispy or Mimi?" Shelley asked Mel.

"Lots of divorces in the first case. Nothing about Mimi except a huge number of parking tickets, which isn't unusual in a college town."

Jane's mind immediately went to Mike. Did this mean she was going to have to budget for parking tickets when he went away to school next year? Who would have thought?

"How about Kathy?" Shelley prodded.

Mel shrugged. "Nothing. Pillars of Oklahoma society. Wild kids in some trouble. One driving without a license charge. Destruction of property after a drinking party. Charges dropped as all the parents made restitution. I don't think you can even embarrass a Southerner with that kind of thing. Lots of them consider it the norm."

"Who's that leave? Only Beth," Jane said.

"She's easy to find out about, but there's nothing questionable," Mel said. "Highly respected judge. A list of civic involvements as long as your arm. All at one remove, it seems."

"What do you mean?" Jane asked.

"Just that she serves on advisory boards, rather than

getting out into the trenches. But that's not so strange in her position. No debts, no marriages or divorces, lives modestly, doesn't drink or smoke. Employs a housekeeper, a gardener, and several law clerks."

"It sounds like you've gone beyond the basics on her," Jane said suspiciously.

"Only because it seemed if blackmail were the trigger, she was a logical one to blackmail. But if anybody found out something to her disadvantage, they've got better investigators than we have," Mel said.

"It didn't seem that Lila was terribly skilled at investigating, just good enough to scratch the surface," Jane said.

"We'd know better about that if we had her notebook," Mel said sourly.

"Mel, I told you—"

"I'm not criticizing. Just saying it might have been helpful."

"Or maybe not. If Crispy's telling the truth, there wasn't anything valuable in it."

"'If' is the operative word. Do you think she's lying?" he directed this question at Shelley.

"You mean, is she capable of lying?" she replied. "Probably. I didn't know her well in high school and I certainly don't know her well now. But why would she need to? If she'd already read the contents, why wouldn't she have been willing to turn the notebook over?"

"Maybe it had something detrimental to her in it." Jane said.

"She could have just torn that page out, if that were the case," Shelley said.

"But that would have been obvious, if she'd turned it over to Mel with one page missing."

"She could have said it was missing when she found

the notebook and while I might not have believed her, I wouldn't have been able to prove otherwise," Mel said.

"Let's assume somebody did take it from her," Jane said. "Where could they have hidden it?"

"It would be easy to hide something in a big, old house like that," Shelley said.

"But we found the pen set easily," Jane said.

"We were meant to," Shelley reminded her. "It was just lying there in an otherwise empty wastebasket. If somebody had really meant to hide it, we might never have found it."

"Why haven't you gotten a search warrant to look for the notebook?" Jane asked Mel.

Mel sighed. "Because they aren't that easy to get, even in a murder case. You see, the crime scene team may define the crime scene as broadly as they want at first. It could include the entire house, the whole block, for that matter. And we can keep the scene sealed for as long as we need to. The law gives us a lot of latitude. If we'd known about this notebook at the time, we could have searched anybody or any-place for it.

"But once the team leaves the area, going back to search puts you in a legal swamp. The defense attorney, when it gets to trial, makes mincemeat of the evidence when you've had to go back for it. That's why we have to be so thorough to start with. And it's why judges are very reluctant to issue search warrants after the crime scene's been unsealed."

"Besides," Jane said wearily, "people had been in and out by the time I remembered to tell you about it. I'm really sorry."

"It might not matter," Mel said generously.

Shelley stood up and stretched. "I've got to go home."

Mel got up, too. He gestured questioningly at the refrigerator. Jane said, "Help yourself. Didn't you get dinner?"

"Not to speak of," he said, opening the refrigerator door and staring in a bewildered manner at the contents.

"Shelley, what's the plan for tomorrow?" Jane asked.

"Oh, I'm glad you asked. I'd forgotten to tell you about breakfast. You don't need to help Edgar in the morning."

"He's not doing breakfast? How are you feeding them?"

"I thought he and you both deserved the morning off. I'm picking up McDonald's breakfasts and bringing them over."

"Edgar must be horrified!" Jane said with a laugh.

"Oh, he is. He says I'll destroy his reputation if I'm seen bringing them into the bed and breakfast. He actually insisted that I put them all in a covered box before I even drive into the neighborhood. But he's also exhausted from the extra strain we've put on him and couldn't make himself turn down the offer. Besides, our class president, Trey Moffat, is hitting him up for another big job."

Mel was unearthing sandwich makings and piling them on the counter and Jane was hoping he didn't find anything revolting enough to ruin their relationship. Given how long it had been since she'd cleaned the fridge, it was possible.

"What job is that?" she asked Shelley.

"The dinner tomorrow."

"But that's at the country club, isn't it?"

"It's supposed to be. But Trey's in a panic. A bunch of people who said they were coming didn't show up. Then about half who did come were so put off by this murder that they're going home after the picnic lunch. Some have already left."

"But he can't cancel the country club this late, can he?"

"Well, there's something odd going on there, too. He thinks the kitchen staff is threatening to strike or something. Anyway, the country club is willing, if not downright eager, to let him off the hook."

"Have you broken this news to Edgar yet?"

"Yes, right after I insisted on bringing in breakfast."

"He's willing?"

"For a really substantial price," Shelley said wryly. "He and Trey are hammering out the details. Thank God that doesn't involve me."

"Why do I have a feeling it *does* involve me?" Jane asked.

"Only a little," Shelley said. "Edgar's doing a buffet. All you're needed for is carrying in an occasional replacement dish when they run low."

Jane groaned. "Do I have to wear a maid's uniform? Maybe one with a short skirt and fishnet hose?"

"You will not! You'll wear that apricot silk dress I made you buy when it was on sale last month."

Jane saluted. "Yes, ma'am. You did promise to loan me your pearls when I wore it."

"Jane, don't you have any mayonnaise?" Mel asked.

"Mel, in a house with teenagers, mayonnaise is The Staff of Life. Keep looking. Okay, Shelley. I'll help drive a load to and from the picnic tomorrow at one o'clock," Jane said, ticking items off on her fingers. "Then dinner duty when?"

"Seven or a little before."

"Then drive one bunch to the airport Sunday morning, right? No changes in that schedule?"

"Lord knows they've tried to change their plans and

get away sooner, but Mel hasn't let them."

Jane glanced at Mel, but the only part of him visible was his back end, bent over, while he rummaged in the fridge. Shelley leaned close to Jane and whispered, "You better get him out of there before he discovers the Biology Drawer. I'm off now. See you tomorrow around one."

Mel emerged victorious with a jar of mayonnaise and told Shelley good-night very cordially before he began constructing his sandwich. Jane sat down and watched with disgust as he put it together.

He caught her look and said, "I have a sergeant who claims that peanut butter is a good investigative tool. He says you can tell where a person is from by what they add to peanut butter sandwiches. Bacon means they came from Philadelphia, bananas mean Memphis or maybe Tupelo. Jelly means different places, depending on the kind of jelly. Grape is Omaha, I think he said. Guava is California and raspberry is Connecticut."

Jane laughed. "And what does mayonnaise and lettuce mean?" she asked as he slapped some rather limp leaves onto his sandwich.

"Outer space," he replied, biting into his construction with a happy grin.

After Mel ate, they sat on the sofa watching an old Jean Harlow movie. Mel had his arm around Jane, and after a while, gently leaned his head on her shoulder. She shivered with anticipation of the nice neck-nuzzle kiss that was coming.

But after a moment she realized his breathing was altogether too regular and even for kissing. He'd fallen asleep. She smiled and snuggled closer, thinking how very comfortable it was to have a sleeping man around again. She didn't really think she wanted it to be a permanent situation, but it was certainly nice for a change.

## 21

On Saturday morning Jane broke down and cleaned out the refrigerator. This was like closing the barn door after the horses had gone, but made her feel better anyway. She'd have to be sure Mel saw the inside of it next time he was here, just so he'd know it didn't always look like it had the evening before. Although, in fact, it usually did.

As always when she did this chore, she found things she had no memory of buying. The red cabbage, for instance. What had she been thinking, getting that? It had rolled back into a corner and turned papery with age. There were the usual sprouting onions and potatoes and a carton of unspeakable cottage cheese. *What if Mel had noticed and opened that*, she thought. The answer was that he'd probably have fallen over, asphyxiated, as she almost did when she discovered it. Even Willard, who considered the refrigerator a veritable feast of odors, had backed away from it.

"Mom, what's that *smell!*" Katie said, stumbling into the kitchen in her nightgown. She picked Max up and cuddled him. Max, who's idea of what was edible was at significant variance from Jane's, meowed to be put back where he could watch for any tasty morsels Jane might unearth.

"A lot of very old things," Jane said. "Why did

somebody put the lunch meat back here without closing the wrapper?"

"Must have been Todd. He's the only one who eats
that yucky stuff," Katie said with a yawn. "It looks
like a frilly hockey puck."

She leaned around Jane and fished a can of tomato
juice out of the refrigerator and took it back upstairs,
presumably to give her strength to begin a strenuous
day of telephoning.

Mike came down a few minutes later, already show-
ered and dressed. He poured himself a gigantic bowl
of cereal and Jane automatically handed him the milk.
"She's already on the phone," he mumbled around the
first mouthful of flakes. Meow was sitting on the chair
opposite, watching him eat.

"I know. Don't give that cat milk *on* the table! What
are you up to today?"

"Scott and I are going to the library, then over to
some school that's having a football game he wants
to see."

"Funny, I didn't think Scott was that crazy about
football," Jane said, sponging off a shelf with baking
soda solution.

"Cheerleader," Mike explained. "You didn't need
me for anything, did you?"

"No, but I need my car."

"It's okay. Scott's driving."

Mike had left and Jane had the refrigerator done
when Elliot's mother called. "Jane, I saw something in
the paper this morning about a county fair that sounds
like fun. We're going to make a day trip of it. Well,
day and night really. We'll probably go to the carnival
in the evening and stay overnight. You don't mind if
Todd comes along, do you?"

"I'd be thrilled. Dorothy, I'll keep them both out of
your hair next weekend."

Jane went upstairs to shower off the stale odor of elderly vegetables, then told Katie she was leaving.

Katie covered the phone with her hand. "Mom! I've got to get a haircut today!"

"You should have said so earlier. I don't have time to take you. I told you I was going to be busy today, remember?"

"Everybody's going to stare at me. I look like a witch!" She flounced her hair to make the point clearer.

"You'll tough it out and be a better person for it," Jane assured her. "Be sure and lock up if you go out."

When she got to the bed and breakfast, nobody seemed in much of a picnic mood, understandably enough. But they'd all decided to go along anyway, because otherwise they would have been trapped at Edgar's all day.

"It's a nice place, but I'm sick of it!" Pooky summed up for them. "I want to go home to my own cooking and my own bathroom."

"Tomorrow," Jane said. "Now, who's riding with me?"

She ended up taking Beth, Avalon, and Pooky. "You all look wonderful," she said cheerfully. Beth and Pooky were in slacks and pretty sweaters; Avalon had on a saggy, baggy dress, but it was a definite red color, unlike her other drab outfits. She had a rolled bandanna around her hair and was wearing a little makeup. It was a clear improvement over her usual appearance. From the proprietary way Pooky was watching her, Jane deduced that Pooky had been responsible for the change.

When they reached the park, the picnic was already

under way. Trey Moffat, the class president, must have been possessed of the same strength of personality as Shelley, because there was a cheerful mood to the gathering in spite of everything. He'd put the men in charge of the cooking at three separate stone fireplaces. The women were scattering around the picnic tables, setting out paper plates and plastic silverware. Jane estimated that he'd managed to coerce nearly seventy or eighty people to attend, not including the children.

"Jane, you're staying, aren't you?" Pooky said as she got out of the car.

"Oh, I don't think so. I'm not needed." She was tempted, though. It had rained overnight, just enough to make everything look clean and fresh. There was a real tang of fall in the air.

"But that's why you ought to stay. You won't have any jobs and there are quite a few single men."

Jane spotted one as Pooky was speaking. Mel was standing by the nearest fireplace, talking to a pudgy, cheerful-looking guy with a fat baby perched on his hip. "Maybe just for a while," Jane said.

The park had originally been a farm. About the time Jane moved into the neighborhood the land, which had been neglected for many years, was acquired by the town and tons of soil brought in and landscaped into pretty rolling hills. Just last year the old homestead building had been renovated into a little historical exhibit. It was only one large room, but partitions with pictures and maps had been put in to divide it up. It nestled cozily at the top of a hill in the midst of a grove of oaks underplanted with old rhododendron hedge. Jane had been inside only once and always meant to get back, but hadn't.

Mel met her as she strolled up the hill toward the

visitor center. "I didn't know you had to be here today," she said.

"Still asking questions. Getting nowhere," he added. "Jane, I'm sorry about last night—"

"You've already apologized and I've told you I didn't mind. You didn't even snore. The way I see it, a man who can fall asleep in the presence of Jean Harlow, let alone me, is *really* tired and deserves a nap."

"Jane, let's go someplace."

"Now? Where?"

"No, when this is over. Anyplace. Just us. There's a nice resort in Wisconsin I've heard about."

Jane stopped in her tracks, trying not to act gauche and stunned. They'd never even made love and he was inviting her for a weekend. The first thing that almost popped out of her mouth was, "But what would my kids think!" but she stopped the words before they escaped.

"Uh—interesting idea. Maybe—" A thousand thoughts were flying around in her head. *Stretch marks*, she thought, panicked. Decent lingerie. Suzie can help with that. Farm out Todd; have to trust Katie and Mike to stay alone without killing each other. Who pays? she wondered. And what *would* she say to the children if she went?

While she'd often been uncomfortable with the fact that she was a few years older than Mel, right now she felt like a child. Which she *was* as far as contemporary social customs were concerned. She'd married young and inexperienced and the world had changed radically before she was widowed. In a way, she was locked into another era, trying to pretend she was part of this one.

"They say there's great fishing and sailing up there,"

Mel was going on. "Peace and quiet and no traffic. How about it?"

"How about getting through the picnic first, and then talking about it?" she said, seeing Shelley approaching.

"Have I offended you?" he asked.

She smiled. "Not at all." *Just jerked me forward a couple of decades,* she thought.

"Hi, Mel," Shelley said. "I want to drag Jane off to meet some people. Do you mind?"

"What were you two talking about? And why are you blushing?" Shelley said as she dragged Jane farther up the hill to a group of people.

"Later—" Jane replied.

She was introduced to a number of people, whose names went right past her. Her mind was already in Wisconsin.

With Mel.

At a resort.

Without children.

Romantic moonlit nights, perhaps some soft music in the background. Loons making their eerie sounds over the still water. The fresh pine-scented air brushing her bare shoulders . . .

Then a dreadful thought crashed this happy reverie. Thelma. Her mother-in-law had been disappointed that Jane hadn't actually constructed a funeral pyre for Steve and thrown herself on it. At least, she'd expected it emotionally, if not physically. Thelma hadn't known that Steve had been leaving Jane for another woman when his car slid on the ice and went into the guardrail. And it probably wouldn't have mattered to her. She still would have expected Jane to grieve for him in virtuous solitude the rest of her life.

*"Jane!"* Shelley pinched her arm. "I want to introduce you to Trey Moffat. You've heard me talk about him."

"Oh, Trey. How nice to meet you," Jane said, rubbing her arm where Shelley had pinched. "You've done a wonderful job organizing."

This was the man Mel had been talking to when Jane first arrived at the picnic. "And you've done a great job helping Shelley, I hear."

As they were speaking, Jane noticed Crispy walking by behind Trey. She was walking slowly, head bent, frowning. That was odd. She hardly looked like herself in such deep repose.

"Would you excuse me for just a second . . . ?" Jane asked and hurried to approach Crispy before she was swallowed by another group of classmates.

"What's up, Crispy?" she asked bluntly.

Her face was pale, and she looked downright haggard. "Oh, Jane. I've figured something out. It's awful. So awful. But it explains almost everything. It was all in the notebook and I just didn't understand—"

"Lila's notebook? The one that disappeared."

"Oh, Jane. You didn't buy that, did you? I didn't leave it where anybody could pick it up."

"You still have it? Why on earth—"

"Ladies, the hot dogs are done to perfection!" Trey Moffat said, catching up with them. "Best in the world. Come along!" He hustled them back down the slope.

"Wait! There's something Crispy and I have to sort out," Jane said.

"It will wait," Crispy said. She glanced at her watch. "Two o'clock. Behind that little house up on the hill," she said. Jane could barely hear her for Trey's blustering about the magnificent job of cooking his group of men had done.

Jane found herself being handed a plate and shoved into a line of people taking potato salad and baked beans. She lost sight of Crispy for a moment, then spotted her talking to Avalon. She still looked preoccupied and sad. Or maybe the expression was anger. Jane glanced around for Mel, thinking she really should report her brief conversation with Crispy to him at the first opportunity, but he wasn't anywhere in sight.

As she sat down with her plate, one of the kids winged a Frisbee down the middle of the table, sending catsup, mustard, and assorted other condiments flying. There were a few minutes of chaos as a result and by the time the miscreant had been caught and sternly admonished and the catsup had been mopped off Jane's blouse, Crispy had disappeared.

Jane abandoned her plate. Shelley was the only familiar face near her now. Jane wriggled through the crowd still surrounding the food table and made her way to where her friend was sitting. "Shelley, have you seen Crispy?"

Shelley caught the alarm in Jane's voice. "She was here a minute ago. I don't know where—"

"Mel. Have you seen Mel?"

"No. What's wrong?"

"I don't know. But I'm worried. Crispy's figured something out. She's mad about it. And now she's disappeared. I need to find Mel."

Shelley stood up. "We'll find him. We'll find both of them. Run over and see if either of them is with that group down at the fireplace near the basketball courts. I'll check the one by the lake."

They tore off in opposite directions. Jane knew she was getting weird looks as she shoved her way through the crowd she was searching with increasing panic. But she didn't care. "Excuse me. Have you

seen Crispy? Have you seen Detective VanDyne?"
she asked of everyone.

But nobody knew who Jane was, few remembered
Crispy, and none acknowledged knowing any detective. As Jane glanced around a last time, she saw
Shelley and Mel hurrying toward her. She ran to meet
them. "I can't find Crispy."

"Jane, what's happened?" Mel asked with hypnotic
calm. "Why are you looking for her?"

Jane took a deep breath. "I spoke to her a few
minutes ago. She said she'd lied about losing the
notebook and she'd figured out what something in
it meant. She said it was something awful."

"What?" Shelley asked.

"There wasn't time for her to tell me. Trey came
up just then and practically dragged us back to eat.
She said to meet her later."

"Where?" Mel demanded.

"Behind the visitor center—the little farmhouse—
up on the hill."

Before Jane had finished speaking, they'd all taken
off running up the hill. "Crispy! Are you there?" Jane
yelled breathlessly as they crested the hill. The three
of them headed around behind the visitor center.

Mel, in better shape, was in the lead. "Not here!"
he shouted back. Jane, trailing, changed course and
rushed in the entrance door at the east end of the
building.

Crispy was sprawled on the floor, her legs and arms
askew as if she were a doll that had been flung down
in a child's rage.

# —— 22 ——

Jane shrieked for Mel as she flung herself toward Crispy. Being careful not to move her limbs or get near the blood pooling beneath her head, Jane gingerly put her fingers to Crispy's neck. She thought there was a pulse, but it could have been the pounding of her own heart echoing in her fingers.

"Run down to the police car in the parking lot," Mel ordered Shelley. "Tell the officer to call for an ambulance and crime scene unit." He knelt on the other side of Crispy and did as Jane had done, touching her throat with his fingers.

"Is she alive?" Jane whispered, her voice clogging in her throat.

"Barely." He put his head down almost on the tiled floor and peered at Crispy intently. He said, "She's been struck hard on the side of the head."

"My God!" Beth said from the west doorway. Because of the partitions that held the displays, they hadn't seen her coming until she rounded the corner.

At the same moment, Pooky came skidding in the east door and gasped at the scene. "We saw you running up here. What's happened?"

"Somebody's tried to kill Crispy," Jane said.

"Ladies, out of the way, please. Each of you take a door and keep everybody out but the medics. Now!" Mel ordered.

Jane knew she shouldn't touch Crispy, but took her hand anyway. "Crispy, hang on. Help is coming," she said, hoping Crispy could hear or sense the comfort. She put the back of Crispy's hand to her cheek. It felt as cold as marble.

Crispy's eyelids fluttered and her lips pursed as if she were attempting to form words. "Mmmmeee—" she said.

Jane leaned closer. "Who did this to you, Crispy?"

"Meet—" Crispy tried again with an enormous effort.

"You met someone. Yes. Who did you meet?"

Crispy tried to shake her head, but her face crumpled in agony at the movement. "Meet. . . . Trey. . . ." she forced out.

"You met Trey?"

"No-o-o—" It began as a word, but ended as a whimpering exhalation.

Jane could hear sirens in the distance and the babble of excited, alarmed conversation outside the building. Above it, she heard Shelley saying very loudly and firmly, "Step back! Get out of the way! The medics need to get through. Clear a path. Harry! Sylvia! Stop dithering around like dummies and get the hell out of the way!"

Suddenly a mob of people in white coats was filling the room, bumping into exhibits, giving orders, clanging around shiny, dangerous-looking equipment. Jane was lifted from the floor and nearly thrown aside. Mel caught her as she crashed against a plastic trash container. She let him hold her up for a moment, then leaned back against the wall, trying not to look at what they were doing to Crispy.

"Come on, Jane. You can't help here," he said.

"I can't leave her," Jane said.

A wiry little blond woman in white had balled her fist and struck Crispy on her breastbone. Jane felt her stomach roll and leaned over the trash barrel to be sick.

But nothing came except a bitter taste at the back of her throat and a rush of freezing sweat on her face and neck. She was afraid to move for fear she'd keel over. Mel came behind her and put a strong arm around her waist, but let her hang there, shaking with horror and shame.

She closed her eyes, breathed deeply, forcing herself to calm down. After a moment, she risked opening her eyes again. Her vision had stopped lurching and swimming. A moment more and she'd stand up. . . .

Among the wads of picnic trash, discarded visitor brochures, and empty soft drink cans in the basket, there was something red. Shiny and red. Even before she plunged her hand in to get it, she knew exactly what it was.

Lila's notebook!

She staggered upright and handed it to Mel. "The notebook," she said, barely trusting herself to speak.

He flipped it open. The yellow pages had been torn out, leaving only a ruffle of ragged paper at the top of the pad. "Shit!" he said as he stuffed it into his pocket.

"Everybody out of the way." One of the medics was pushing the two of them toward the east door. Four others were gently lifting Crispy onto a gurney. She had a tube in her throat, tubes running into her arms, wires seemingly snarled all over. The three burliest men surrounded the gurney and started angling it out the west door. One held two bottles of liquid aloft. Another was running sideways and rhythmically

squashing a rubber bellows that connected to a tube
that went down Crispy's throat.

Jane leaned against Mel and sobbed.


"I'm all right," she said testily to Shelley. "Really!
Now stop fussing over me."

"Getting nasty, huh?" Shelley said, setting a fresh
cup of coffee in front of her. They were sitting at
Jane's kitchen table.

"I hate to admit this, but I don't exactly *know* how
I got home," Jane said.

"I drove you."

"I thought so, but I wasn't certain. Where's my car?
What did you do with the rest of them?"

"Your car will be brought along whenever a couple
of officers are free to bring it. With the help of the
police, I stuffed the others into cabs and sent them
back to Edgar's. I seriously considered drowning them
all and being done with this, but there were too many
cops around."

"Edgar must be berserk by now. At least he won't
have to throw the party tonight, even though he's
probably made all the food already." Jane knew she
was meandering mentally, but it seemed a pleasant
alternative to thinking about Crispy.

Shelley stirred her coffee. "That's not exactly true.
About the party."

"Shelley! You can't mean the party is still going to
happen! Is Trey crazy?"

"No, Trey's on the very brink of being arrested.
And the party has become an inquest or inquisition or
something. It's not a party anymore. It's a place where
all the suspects and witnesses and possible witnesses
have been told to show up if they value their freedom."

"Trey," Jane said. "Crispy said she was going to

meet Trey. Or I was supposed to meet him. I don't know what she meant."

"I couldn't hear her," Shelley said. "What were her exact words?"

Jane took a gulp of coffee. Too big a gulp. It scalded her mouth slightly. But the pain seemed to clear her mind. "She said 'Meet' and I asked who she'd met. And she said 'Meet Trey.' And I said something like, 'Did you meet with Trey?' and she said, 'no.' And that's all she said. Shelley, was she alive when they took her away?"

"I don't know. I think she must have been or they wouldn't have been in such a rush to get her to the hospital."

"Could we call the hospital and ask? Do you know where she was taken?"

"I tried already while you were in the bathroom chucking up everything you've ever eaten in your life. They wouldn't give me a hint. They just said it was a police matter and to make my inquiries through them."

"Then let's do that."

"Jane, you know Mel will call you as soon as he can. And nobody else in the department would tell you anything. Tell me again. Exactly what did Crispy say?"

Jane repeated what she'd already told her and added, "I don't get it. When I asked her if she'd met with Trey, she tried to shake her head and she definitely said 'no.' So why was she talking about Trey at all? What could he possibly have to do with this?"

"I can't imagine."

"Maybe she wanted *me* to meet him. Maybe she'd told him something she wanted me to know, but didn't have the strength to tell me herself."

"I don't think so. At least, when I eavesdropped on Mel questioning him, he vehemently denied having had any conversation with her at all."

"But that's not true," Jane said. "I was talking to her when he came up and hustled us to the food. He spoke to both of us. In fact, he was just dragging us into the mob when she told me to meet her behind the visitor center."

"Hmmm. So he either lied, or he just snagged the two of you without paying any attention to who you were. I think that's more likely."

"Why?"

Shelley considered. "Because he's too dumb and nice to lie well. And because he was genuinely horrified at being questioned and was spilling his guts to every question. And because he's a minister." She said the last with a self-mocking smile. "I know that ministers *can* lie. But they're marginally less likely to, I'd think."

"Didn't anybody see him with us? How did they know to question him at all?"

"I don't know. Maybe just because he was in charge of the picnic. Or maybe someone did see him dragging you two to the festivities. I didn't get in on the beginning of the questioning and one of Mel's minions noticed me snooping and ran me off before I could learn anything more."

The phone rang and Jane nearly upset her chair as she leaped to answer it. "Oh, Katie. Yes. No, there's nothing wrong. I just tripped. Okay, but come get your things right now while I'm home so I can lock up after you."

"She's spending the night with Jenny," Jane said to Shelley. She glanced at the kitchen clock. "Quarter after three. What time do I have to be back at Edgar's?"

"Never."

"Why? Has he hired more help?"

"No, but I'll help. We can manage."

"Shelley, I'm not an invalid. I'm really fine."

"Then why do you look so dopey?"

"Do I?" She thought for a minute. "I have this weird feeling that I know something I don't know. I've had it since we talked last night."

"When did it start?" Shelley asked. It was a measure of their long friendship that Shelley understood the feeling Jane was floundering around in.

"I think it was when we were talking about what each of them had to lose and were doing a sort of minianalysis of each one. There's something you said about one of them and a few minutes later, I thought, 'That's not true and I know it.' But I can't bring it back—"

"Which one?" Shelley asked.

"That's the problem. I don't remember. But it's one of those things like Pooky being stupid."

"She's not?"

"It was an example. I don't know if it was Pooky or somebody else. And there's something about that yearbook that Mimi brought along that keeps nudging at the back of my mind. Maybe if I'd look at it again—"

"Leave it alone," Shelley advised. "If you don't consciously try to capture it, it might pop into your head. Things usually do."

"I wish we knew about Crispy. Uh-oh. Here comes Katie. If Hazel comes to the door, tell her I'm in the shower. I couldn't stand to talk to her right now."

Fortunately Jenny's mother stayed in the car and Katie ran through the house and upstairs without saying anything but hello in passing. A moment later, she was on her way out carrying enough clothing to live at Jenny's for a month. "Jenny's going to cut my hair for me, Mom," she said as she flew by.

"It'll grow out," Shelley told Jane when the door slammed. "And if not, wigs have really come down in price lately."

"Isn't that my car coming down the street?"

"With Mel's car following."

They were in the driveway by the time Jane's station wagon wallowed over the curbing and came to rest. The officer got out and handed Jane the keys, but her attention was on Mel.

"Tell us," she said.

"She's alive. But she's on life-support."

"But she *is* alive!" Jane said.

"Jane, don't get your hopes up. It looks like she's sustained massive brain trauma. Her chances of surviving, much less ever waking up, are very remote."

"May I see her?"

"Of course not," he snapped. Then, "I'm sorry. But you can't. I have to go." The other officer had crammed his considerable bulk into the passenger seat of Mel's red MG and looked enormously uncomfortable.

"I know," Jane said. "Go."

She almost added that she'd see him at Edgar's later, but decided it would be better not to mention that in advance.

# — 23 —

Shelley met Jane at the kitchen door of the bed and breakfast as Jane came in. Hector had already met her in the driveway and shot into the house between her feet. "Decided against the silk dress, I see," Shelley said sarcastically.

"It seemed a bit festive for the occasion." Jane was wearing a denim skirt and a camel-colored sweater Mike had outgrown.

"You look like a bag lady."

"No, I look like Avalon." She shoved her purse into the cabinet next to the back door. Hector tried to squirm in and investigate the cabinet, but she pulled him out, protesting loudly. "So, how bad is it?" she asked Shelley.

"About as bad as you'd expect. Mel's in the dining room, interviewing people. Everybody else is milling around in the living room. There are about fifteen of us, excluding the police. But only the five remaining Ewe Lambs are suspects."

"Not really," Jane said. "I was thinking about it on the way over. You and I are officially on the list even though Mel certainly knows we didn't do it. And there are two others who have been present for the duration of the reunion. Let's sit down for a minute. I can't face it yet."

Jane absentmindedly wandered the kitchen, looking

at the food that was almost ready to be served. In spite of the morbid circumstances, Edgar had put on a feast. There were stuffed lamb chops, scalloped potatoes with a faint rosemary smell, a braised celery dish, a cold beet salad with sour cream and dill, and a cauliflower concoction that looked as if it had been parboiled and marinated in a spicy dressing. For those with a lesser appetite, there was a melon boat, cold meats and cheeses, and rye rolls. The food smelled wonderful, but Jane couldn't have eaten a bite.

Shelley poured two cups of Edgar's remarkable coffee and they sat down at the kitchen table. Jane lighted a cigarette. Hector, curled in the chair opposite her, gave a disdainful look of disapproval.

"Who are the other two?" Shelley asked. "What did you mean by that?"

Jane lowered her voice almost to a whisper. "Edgar and Gordon."

"You don't think—"

"No, I don't. But we've been pretty dumb to discount them entirely and you know Mel must be considering them."

"But they had no previous connection with the Ewe Lambs."

"—that you know of."

"Oh, Jane. I wish you'd never said this. I think I'm going mad! Oh, you'll love this: there are two couples here who actually believe this is a party. They came voluntarily!"

"No."

"Yes. An accountant and some twit who works for a consumer advocacy group. They put their pointy little heads together and decided that they'd paid for a reunion banquet and By God, they were going to attend one, come hell or high water. The accountant has a wife along who looks like she's hunting for a rock to crawl under. Oh, and Pooky's plastic surgeon friend came. He didn't have to, but came for Pooky's sake. Which I think is sweet."

"It looks like one person has come out ahead. I'm glad. Did Mel say anything else about Crispy's condition?"

"Just that she's still hanging on. He did mention that they found the weapon. A heavy stick from those woods behind the building. It must have been a perfect club, heavy, close at hand, and easy to dispose of."

"Fingerprints?"

"No. The bark was too rough."

"Anything about the notebook?"

"Mel said the prints were wiped off," Shelley reported.

"Shelley, I keep trying to imagine what happened before we got there. Crispy must have had the notebook with her and confronted somebody with what she'd learned."

"Presumably."

"But who tore the pages out?"

"Her attacker. Who else would? She probably ran into that little rest room at the visitor center and flushed them."

"Not likely. Think about the timing. If her attacker had lots of leisure time, she'd have made sure she'd finished Crispy off."

"That's right. Why didn't she?"

"Maybe because we were running up the hill yelling. And even if she didn't hear *us* coming, she had to have known that anybody could have walked in any second just to have a look around. She didn't have a lot of time. Just enough to club Crispy, grab the notebook, wipe off her fingerprints, shove it in the trash, and get the hell away from the place. Tearing out pages and flushing them would have taken even more time. And I don't think a toilet was running when I got in there, although I admit I wasn't noticing much of anything but Crispy, and I might not have been able to hear it anyway with all those display walls in the building."

"Yes, but what conclusion does that lead you to, Jane? That the attacker ripped the pages out and took them along?"

"That's one possibility. She could have easily slipped them into one of the barbecue fires. But I was really thinking of Crispy herself. Look, Shelley, Crispy kept the notebook for some stupid reason. To wave around in somebody's face, maybe? But wouldn't she take the pages out and put them somewhere safe first?"

Shelley leaned back in her chair and tented her fingers. "Hmmm. Are you suggesting that Crispy wanted to use Lila's notebook for blackmail, too?"

"Not blackmail exactly. Not to get anything from anybody. But Crispy liked embarrassing people. Remember, I told you when I first met her at the airport, she said she intended to torment the other Ewe Lambs. Remind them of foolish things they'd done. Make them feel silly. I guess as some kind of revenge for not liking her and including her in high school."

"Okay, so assuming she kept the notebook—you're probably right, she might well have torn the pages out. But where would she have put them? The police went over her room with a fine-tooth comb. They were still here when I came back."

"No, she knew the rooms wouldn't lock and two of them had already been searched."

"Then where would she put them?"

"I have no idea."

"Jane! You're here. Thank heaven," Edgar said, bustling into the kitchen with a tray of dirty glasses.

Jane leaped to her feet. "I'm sorry. I should be helping."

"Make an ashtray run, would you?" Edgar said. He was rinsing out glasses and stacking them in the dishwasher.

Jane picked up the decorative metal canister Edgar used to empty ashtrays into and went to the living room.

It was about the gloomiest gathering she'd ever walked into. The air was blue with smoke, in spite of the fact that someone had opened one of the French doors. People were sitting around in dispirited clumps, barely speaking. There were only two islands of brightness. One was Pooky and her friend sitting close together on a sofa, chattering happily. The other was a group around Trey Moffat and his pretty wife and smiling baby. She was holding the infant and Trey was making baby talk and prodding it, making it laugh. The baby's laugh was so infectious that the group around them was smiling.

Jane strolled around, picking up ashtrays and eavesdropping. Mimi was chatting with another woman about the schedule of a traveling art exhibit. Beth was having a discussion on managing clerks' billing hours with a man who was presumably also an attorney. Kathy was talking about capital gains with the accountant. Avalon was sitting by herself, knitting as if her life depended on finishing the garment.

Jane took the canister back through the kitchen and set it outside the back door. Edgar was getting out the food in preparation for serving. He'd put the long library table at the north end of the living room earlier and covered it with a white lace cloth. "Did I remember the napkins out there?" he said as he wrestled an enormous container of deviled eggs out of the refrigerator.

"I'll check," Jane said. She peeked around the door. "Yes, they're on the table."

"Okay, I'll take the melon out. Hold the door for me, then bring the meat and cheese tray."

Jane held the door for him, then picked up the tray she was to bring. She edged through the door carefully. The thing wasn't heavy, but it was large and awkward. She followed Edgar through the room and said, "Where do you want the meat tray?"

"At the other end."

"Meat tray. . . ." Jane repeated. "Meat tray!"

She nearly dropped it.

Could Crispy have been saying "meat tray" not "meet Trey"?

And if so, what the hell could it mean?

Jane went back to the kitchen and got more dishes to carry in, all the while mumbling to herself. Were there other variations? Meat? Did meat have any significance? Or tray? She made a third trip and a fourth and went back to the kitchen. The counter was now clear. Nothing else to take in. She leaned back against the refrigerator for a moment, thinking furiously.

Her eyes opened very wide and she turned around to stare at the fridge. She pulled on the door, wondering if Edgar's super-duper appliance had the same features as hers. Yes, indeed it did! A shallow drawer under the middle shelf meant for keeping meats. *A meat tray.*

But Edgar kept flat boxes of Godiva chocolates in it. Jane pulled the drawer out as far as it would go and started lifting out the gold boxes of candy. At the back, under the last box, was a little stack of yellow sheets of paper.

Jane grabbed the papers, glanced through, and shoved them into the pocket of her skirt. Then she hastily put the candy back and closed the door. She went back to the living room, where people were milling around the library table, serving themselves dinner. Shelley and Trey had been cornered by the accountant and the consumer rights advocate, who were giving them hell about the nature of the "banquet" and the money they'd paid for it.

"Excuse me," Jane said. "Shelley, I need to talk to you."

"Now, just a minute, little lady," the accountant said. "We got us some business to talk over with Shelley. You're gonna have to hold your horses."

Jane stepped back, fished the papers out of her pocket and held them up for Shelley to see. Shelley's eyes went saucerlike. "I'm afraid it's *your* horses that are going to have to wait, Lloyd," she said, pushing past him. "Put those away before somebody sees them," Shelley hissed as she took Jane's arm and hurried her to the library. She slammed the door behind them and said, "Let me see!"

## 24

Jane laid the papers out on an end table next to the sofa and turned on the lamp. At first glance they didn't seem to mean much of anything. Same names, numbers, many items crossed out. Some starred.

"I have to give them to Mel right away."

"Right!" Shelley said. She went to the corner where the copier and fax stood and turned on the copier. "Lay them out," she said.

They made two copies and Shelley stayed behind while Jane went to the dining room. She tapped on the door and opened it. "Detective VanDyne—"

Mel was sitting across the table from Trey Moffat's wife, who looked like a rabbit caught in someone's headlights. "Mrs. Jeffry, I'm busy at the moment," Mel said sharply. "If you could wait outside for—"

"I'm sorry, but it really can't wait." Jane came into the room and handed him the yellow sheets.

He looked down at them, then at her. "Where did you find these?"

"In the refrigerator. In the M-E-A-T T-R-A-Y."

He smiled at her. "Good. Good! Thank you, Mrs. Jeffry."

She all but danced back to the library. Shelley was sitting on the sofa, staring at one of the two copies they'd made. By overlapping the pages, they'd gotten the information from all six small sheets of yellow paper on one page.

Shelley handed Jane the second copy. "She did a nice job of being obscure. If you didn't know what these meant, you'd never guess, and some still don't make sense."

Jane studied her sheet. "There isn't one for Crispy."

"She must have destroyed her own page."

Under Avalon's name was a long number and ARK with a date following it. A couple of telephone numbers had been crossed out. "That must be a case number or something for the charge about the drugs," Jane said. "Possibly the date the case was filed, or the date the charges were made."

"And the telephone numbers are probably the foster care agencies she contacted. I'll bet the starred number is the one where she actually got the information she was looking for. None of the pages have more than one number starred."

"Pooky's looks pretty much the same."

"Kathy's is the easiest," Shelley said. "It's a list of stock abbreviations and I imagine the figures that follow are the number of shares Kathy has. What are the telephone numbers? Brokers, probably. If nothing else, the police are going to ask the people at these numbers some pretty awkward questions about how Lila got confidential information."

"What do you suppose Beth's means?" Jane asked.

Beth's entry said "S. Francisco—Dr. Page—Admissions" and a telephone number with a California area code followed.

"A hospital, it looks like. What would Beth have to do with a hospital?" Shelley asked.

"A mental hospital, maybe. A breakdown?" Jane wondered.

"And what does Mimi's mean?" Mimi's entry said "St. Vincent's—admission date?—b.cert." and some crossed out telephone numbers followed it. "If starred numbers mean success in getting the information, she didn't get what she wanted on Mimi," Shelley said.

"Shelley, could you please talk to Lloyd!" Trey Moffat said from the doorway. He was jiggling the baby, who was starting to look tired and cranky.

They hadn't heard him open the door. Jane and Shelley hastily folded and concealed the papers they'd been studying. "Oh, Trey, just smack him, why don't you?" Shelley snapped. "This party is your problem, not mine."

"C'mon, Shelley! The police are grilling my wife! Help me out here!" Trey's good nature had finally run out.

"Okay, but you aren't going to like what I say to him," Shelley said, getting up and rejoining the group in the living room. Not being especially eager to see bloodshed, Jane stayed back, opened her sheet of paper again, and studied it for a few moments without making any more sense of it. Slipping it back into her pocket, she wandered out to the living room.

Lloyd was sitting down next to the television with a plate of food on his knees. His wife was fussing over him and trying to conceal a smile. He looked like he'd been hit between the eyes with a brick. Shelley must have laid some pretty brutal truths on him. Shelley herself was calmly serving herself from a casserole of scalloped potatoes and chatting with Avalon and Edgar. *Much as Attila the Hun must have done after a day of looting and pillaging,* Jane thought to herself.

Mrs. Moffat had been turned loose from the glare of police attention and seemed enormously relieved. She was sitting on the sofa next to Trey, playing pat-a-cake with the baby and making syrupy cooing noises. Pooky was sitting on the other side of Mrs. Moffat, laughing. Pooky's new friend was standing over her, his hand on her shoulder. Jane was drawn to this pleasant circle. She sat down in the chair at right angles to the sofa.

She had it. She knew somewhere deep in her sub-conscious all this made sense. If she could just pull out the right pieces and make them fit together.

"Is he headed for the ministry, too?" Pooky's friend asked Trey.

"If he wants," Trey said, putting his arm around his cute little wife and smiling idiotically at the baby. "Or the law, or medicine. My only responsibility will be to see that he gets into the best college that money or bribery can buy!" He laughed uproariously.

"What did you say?" Jane asked, sitting forward so suddenly she nearly upset the coffee table with her knee.

"Oh, it was just a joke, Mrs. Jeffry!" Trey said, alarmed that she might have taken him seriously. It seemed he'd just realized that ministers shouldn't make jokes about indulging in illegal activities.

"Yes. I know. The best college . . ."

"Are you all right?" Trey asked her.

"Yes, fine. Fine. I just—Pooky, what was Ted's father's first name?"

"Ted's dad? The judge? I have no idea. No, let me think—Samuel, maybe. Or Steven. No, it was Samuel. Why?"

"S. Francisco—" Jane muttered.

If she'd only paid closer attention to something her son Mike had said, she'd have figured it out long ago.

*If* she was right. . . .

If *Lila* was right.

Jane fished the folded paper out of her pocket, excused herself, and went to the kitchen. Fortunately, nobody was there but Hector, who was sitting on a chair, stretching his neck to look at the counter. Jane reached for the phone and punched in the California telephone number that had the star next to it. After four endless rings, a machine picked up. "This is the admissions office of Stanford University. Our office hours are—"

Jane hung up the phone. Hector said, "Brbrbreow!" She scratched his ears absently. Yes. Not a hospital. "Admissions" didn't mean a hospital. It meant a college. And "S. Francisco" didn't mean San Francisco, it meant Samuel Francisco, the judge who hadn't approved of Beth dating her son, but had inexplicably given her a glowing recommendation that had eliminated the final hurdle to her getting a full scholarship.

Or so Lila had told someone.

Jane paced for a moment and suddenly stopped in her tracks, her mind dashing in sixteen directions at once. *Calm down,* she told herself, closing her eyes. *One thing at a time.*

The recommendation was a forgery, just as Mike had jokingly suggested for himself days ago. Ted, still enamored of Beth, had probably stolen some of his father's stationery for her and might have supplied something with Judge Francisco's signature. And Beth had sailed into college on a full scholarship. Not that she hadn't deserved it, but a judge who had gotten an education predicated in part on a forged document would not only fail to get to the Supreme Court, she'd probably be disbarred. But there wasn't any way to prove it. Judge Francisco was dead now. Still, there were handwriting analysts who could prove the case without him. Even if it were never proved, the scandal would destroy her life's work.

Jane had to tell Mel right away.

She turned and found herself face-to-face with Beth.

"I think we better go outside," Beth said calmly.

She had one of Edgar's carving knives in her hand and touched the tip of the blade to Jane's sweater.

"You forged the recommendation, didn't you? That's what all this has been about!"

"Is that what was on those little yellow papers you were carrying around? Crispy was stupid to tear them out and leave them around for a busybody like you to find. Hand them over."

"I don't have them."

"Then let's go outside and you can tell me where you put them." Her voice was eerily calm.

*If she gets me outside, I'm dead,* Jane thought. *I have to stop her inside. But how?* An idea skittered through her brain and she latched onto it. It wasn't a good idea, but it was the only one she had.

Hector, unaware of the danger, was stropping himself against Jane's legs.

"You could have," she stopped. Coughed. "—have paid her off, (cough, cough) you know. Even if you didn't, it would have ruined your career, but you (cough) wouldn't have gone to jail (cough, cough, cough) for forging the recommendation."

"Pay her off for the rest of my life? Let's go outside and discuss this in the carriage house. Now!" She pressed the knife through the sweater and into Jane's skin just beneath her breastbone.

Jane gritted her teeth. *The carriage house!*

*It wasn't just forgery,* she realized. It was more. Far more! Had Lila figured that out? Or had Beth only feared that she would eventually?

Faking the cough wasn't so hard now. She could hardly breathe for fear. "When you broke up (cough, cough, cough) with Ted, he was humiliated and threatened (cough) to tell his father, didn't he? (cough, cough) You couldn't afford (cough) to have that happen. You're the one who started the car (cough, cough) after he fell into bed (cough) dead drunk. You killed Ted."

"Why, you're smarter than you look. Now, move!"

"Wait! I'll (cough, cough) tell you where the notes are. Just let me (cough) get a (cough, cough, cough) drink of water. It's that cat (cough). I'm allergic. Please."

"Make it fast!"

Still hacking and coughing, Jane cracked the refrigerator door, shoving Hector out of the way with her foot at the same time. The door opened toward Beth. Jane glanced inside and gasped in horror.

Instinctively, Beth leaned forward to see what Jane was looking at, and as she did so, Jane jerked the door open with all her might. It swung around, hitting Beth squarely in the face.

The knife clattered to the floor as Beth fell backward, her hands to her face. Blood was pouring from her nose and she was making a gurgling, screaming sound as she hit the floor and started scrambling for the knife.

Jane dived for the floor, too, and got to the knife first. Beth swung at her, blood splattering everywhere.

Doors flew open and the room was suddenly full of horrified witnesses. Shelley did a running long jump over Beth to reach Jane.

"My God! Jane is this your blood?" she asked, squatting down on the floor next to her.

Jane took a deep, trembling breath and hung onto

Shelley. "I don't know. I don't think so." Mel had pushed through the crowd and was holding Beth's arm and mechanically advising her of her rights, but he was looking intently at Jane.

Jane looked at Beth, whose face was twisted with fury and despair. "In a way, it's Ted's blood. . . ."

## 25

"Not the cream puffs again," Jane groaned. "I've probably gained a ton this week. No, Edgar. Set them a little closer to me, would you?"

It was Sunday evening. The bed and breakfast was Ewe Lamb–less, except for Shelley. Edgar, who should have been taking a well-deserved rest, had insisted on serving a big dinner to Jane and her family, Shelley and her children, and Mel. The meal consisted almost entirely of leftovers from the night before, but Edgar's leftovers were better that Jane's first-timers, as she told him.

Dinner was over now and the children were in the living room with the Nintendo. Edgar was not only a superior cook, he also had a better selection of games than Jane did. There were several she intended to try before the day was over.

Mel had left the dining room between dinner and dessert and now came back. "Crispy's been taken off life-support," he said.

"No! Who gave that order?" Jane asked.

"Calm down. It doesn't mean what you think. She's off because she's breathing on her own. The doctor says she must either have enormous determination to live or a cast iron brain. They think she may even regain consciousness." He popped a mini–cream puff in his mouth and practically swallowed it whole. "I

208

don't suppose there's any hope that you made this, Jane?"

"Afraid not."

"That's too bad. The odd thing is," he went on, "there are not one but two of Crispy's ex-husbands pacing the hall driving the nurses crazy. How did they find out? And why did they contact each other?"

"They probably have a support group," Shelley said. "With a 1-800 number."

"I don't suppose Beth's admitted anything?" Jane asked.

"She hasn't uttered a syllable except to remind us that it's our responsibility to build a case and she won't contribute to our efforts," Mel said. "But that's all right. We've identified fibers from the rags in the carriage house on the clothing Beth was wearing the night she killed Lila. That proves she was at the murder site and actually came in contact with the fabric Lila's body was covered up with. If Crispy does wake up, we'll have her testimony as well. I don't know that we'll ever prove Beth's role in Ted Francisco's death. It's too long ago and the physical evidence is ancient. But we'll certainly nail her on Lila's. She's also got splinters in her palm that will match with the branch she used as a club, but the legal eagles are having a row about the legality of removing them."

"Jane, remember when you were talking about us being wrong in our assessment of somebody?" Shelley asked. "Did you ever remember what it was?"

"Oh, yes. As Beth was ruining my sweater with that knife. It was her self-control. Legendary, almost. Everybody, including us, kept saying how she never lost her cool in her life. But I saw her go entirely to pieces."

"The deodorant!" Edgar said, crinkling his nose in remembrance of the smell.

"Right. She was running around in the upstairs hall, practically naked, having hysterics. I'm not sure that even I would have gone *that* nuts. So there was a gaping hole in her legendary self-possession."

"You think she just went berserk when she killed Lila?" Shelley asked.

"Maybe. It was a very violent act, hitting her with the paint can. And hitting Crispy with that stick."

"What *was* Mrs. Morgan doing letting herself be caught alone with a killer?" Gordon asked. So far he'd been silent throughout dinner and their discussion.

"We don't know," Shelley said. "Maybe she just went there early to meet Jane and Beth caught up with her."

"But it still doesn't make sense. The place had two doors. Why didn't she just run like hell?" Shelley asked.

"Possibly because she'd made the same leap I did from the fake recommendation to Beth's killing Ted to keep it secret. Crispy loved Ted," Jane said. "Not just a crush like the rest of the Ewe Lambs, but real love, I think. In fact, I would guess that deep down inside, she still loves him and may have cast off all those husbands for the simple reason that none of them were Ted. Imagine, all these years she's probably beaten herself up over his 'suicide.' Thinking that if she'd been a better friend, she could have seen it coming, or talked him out of it, or something. People do that when somebody they love takes his own life."

Shelley nodded. "And if she figured out that Beth had killed him—"

"She'd have been so furious that she might have thrown caution to the winds. Maybe she forgot or ignored the threat to herself in her eagerness to tell Beth what a vile person she was."

"But keeping the notebook was so stupid," Edgar said. "Why didn't she just turn it over to the police?"

Shelley spoke up. "My guess would be because she wanted to have the leisure to ferret out what it all meant first. It probably didn't occur to her that there was a copier right in the house. She'd only been in the library for our meeting and she sat with her back to it."

"It still doesn't make sense," Gordon put in. "Why would she need to figure it out herself? The police were already working on the case."

"I think it was partly because she honestly believed she was smarter than the police," Jane said.

"A trait shared by a number of people," Mel said.

Jane ignored his sarcasm. "I think it was mainly because she was basically an extraordinarily snoopy person. She wanted to know what Lila had on people. She might or might not have ever used the information to humiliate them, but she just *had* to know."

"Like my sister-in-law, Constanza," Shelley said.

"Exactly. Mel? Do you know yet what the notes about Mimi meant?"

"Yes, that was an easy one. Her first child is institutionalized. He's severely retarded."

"Was Lila trying to hold that over her?"

"She might have intended to, but she never got around to it or she didn't get her facts lined up in time," Mel said. "She would have been unpleasantly surprised if she had. Mrs. Soong was very open about it. She said she doesn't bring it up because it upsets other people, who don't know what to say to her, but it's never been a secret."

Edgar pushed the cream puff tray closer to Jane,

who snatched another one. Edgar asked, "I know you and Shelley had the notes Lila had made, but how did you guess what the ones on Beth meant?"

Much as Jane was enjoying the chance to show off her cleverness, she wished they'd quit asking questions so she could apply herself seriously to the cream puffs. "I heard Trey Moffat make a joke about bribery being a means of getting his baby into a good college."

"I certainly wouldn't have made that leap of logic," Edgar said.

"That's because you're not deep in the agony of getting a kid into college. Just the other day my son Mike was bemoaning the fact that he didn't have anybody important and influential to write him a recommendation and he said, as a joke, that he didn't need to know them, all he needed was some of their stationery. Both Trey Moffat and my son are highly honorable people, but even they recognize that it may take less than honorable means to get into a good school.

"Then I remembered a conversation with Mimi. She'd said Lila mentioned that Beth had gotten a great college recommendation letter from Judge Francisco. Mimi was surprised by that, saying that the Franciscos hadn't really approved of Beth."

"I didn't know about a letter of recommendation. Not at the time," Shelley said.

"No, none of you would have. Beth wasn't a bragger and she was very close with information about herself. She wouldn't have told any of you about the letter then, even if it had been legitimate. So, I reasoned that if Lila knew about it, she had to have found out by herself as part of her blackmail campaign preparation. Then the notes she'd made about Beth made sense."

"I guess so," Edgar admitted. "But why the silly

practical jokes? Why would someone like Beth play such stupid tricks?"

"Only two of them were her doing. And they weren't jokes at all."

Mel looked at her with surprise. They'd talked about the murder the night before, but not the practical jokes. "What do you mean?"

"This is just a guess, mind you, but Beth was worried about that picture Avalon drew."

"The picture she gave me?" Edgar asked uneasily.

"Avalon said she did it the night Ted died. And it was full of little secret figures. I think Beth was terrified that *she* was in the picture someplace. That Avalon might have seen her leaving after she started Ted's car. Avalon said she heard the car start and ran away. But what if she hadn't gone immediately? So Beth wanted to find and destroy the picture."

"That's why she searched Avalon's room!" Shelley said. "But why did she wait so long to do it?"

"Because she searched Pooky's room first. Remember how determined Pooky was to have the picture? I was surprised when Edgar showed it to me. I assumed Avalon had caved in and given it to Pooky. Beth probably made the same assumption. So she tore up Pooky's room looking for it."

"And stole the antique?" Mel said doubtfully.

"Just to make it look like it was part of the spate of jokes. Keep in mind that she 'hid' it where we could hardly keep from finding it."

"And by the time she got to Avalon's room, she was getting frantic enough not to bother," Shelley said.

"Probably."

Gordon got up and started stacking plates to take to the kitchen.

"And which of the Ewe Lambs did the other jokes?" Mel asked. He still looked skeptical.

"Gordon, don't take those dishes just yet," Jane said. "Come back. You'll find this interesting."

"You think so?" he asked with a smile.

Jane spoke to Shelley. "Who in your high school class was a practical joker?"

"Why—nobody that I know of."

"You're sure? What about Gloria Kevitch?"

"Gloria who? Oh, yes. I do remember. She was always in trouble over something. How do *you* know her name?"

Edgar mumbled an exclamation and looked at Gordon. So did Mel.

"Is this another Ewe Lamb we're talking about?" Mel asked.

"No, she wasn't a Ewe Lamb," Shelley said.

"She's the girl the high school yearbook was dedicated to," Jane explained. "Mimi said Gloria Kevitch had applied to be a Ewe Lamb but was turned down. Later on, she died in a car accident. Maybe a suicide, maybe an accident."

"Jane, you've lost your mind," Shelley said. "What on earth could all this possibly have to do with what happened here? Unless you're suggesting that poor little Gloria has come back to haunt the Ewe Lambs. I don't believe you'll ever convince me of that!" she added with a laugh.

"Oh, but she did haunt you. Didn't she, Gordon?"

He was sitting next to Edgar now, drawing patterns on the tablecloth with his fork. He finally looked up at Jane. "You're kind of spooky yourself," he said. "How did you know?"

"I brought in your mail and sorted it into piles."

Gordon nodded. "And something came to me as Kevitch. I see."

"*Kevitch?*" Shelley exclaimed.

"I presume you only use Kane as your professional name," Jane said.

"Yes, I never legally changed it. But I've been using Kane ever since my first art showing. Gloria was so hurt by being rejected by the Ewe Lambs. I don't mean that she killed herself over it, but it was one of many contributing factors. And she did love practical jokes." He smiled. "When Edgar told me who this group was, well—it just seemed like poetic justice."

"I get it! That's why the jokes weren't very good ones," Shelley said. "Sorry, Gordon, but they weren't, you know. Because they were being done by somebody who didn't really have a feel for the art form. *You* didn't go to school with us, did you?"

"Same school, about six years earlier."

"Gordon!" Edgar exclaimed. "How *could* you!"

"I didn't hurt anybody or damage anything. And it was fun!"

"I meant, how could you not tell me?" Edgar clearly had his feelings hurt.

"Because you'd have told me to be sensible and stop horsing around."

"No, I wouldn't—"

Mel caught Jane's eye and gestured toward the door.

The argument was still raging and Shelley had jumped into it with both feet when Mel took Jane's hand and led her past the children and out onto the patio. They sat down on a wooden bench that encircled an old oak tree.

"My mother would call you one smart cookie," Mel said.

"Would she? What would you call me?"

He leaned back against the tree. "An idiot maybe. An interfering busybody with no more sense of self-preservation than a lemming." Without looking at her, he took her hand and kneaded it between his. "Jane, you know I've seen a lot of awful things. But I swear, I've never seen anything that scared me as much as when I came in the kitchen last night and saw you sitting there covered with blood."

"I'm sorry. I really am."

"—and that's why I'm taking back my invitation to go to Wisconsin."

"Oh. . . . I see. . . ."

"No, you don't. I meant the weekend for my sake. Sexy fun and games with a little fishing and 'guy' stuff thrown in for good measure. I was being a selfish bastard."

Jane didn't know what to say, and, for once in her life, had the wits to keep quiet.

"So I want to start over. I'd like to take you some-place *you'd* like to go. New York, maybe? Take in some shows? See the Statue of Liberty? Window-shop?"

Jane was relieved and flattered, but still faced the same problems as she had with the original invitation. "Mel, I'd like to, but I'm afraid."

He looked at her sharply. "Afraid of me?"

"Afraid of disappointing you. Yes, that's one of the things I'm afraid of."

"Jane, you couldn't disappoint me if you worked at it."

"Mel, I've been in a time capsule for nearly twenty years. I don't know anything about . . . about having an affair. I don't have the underwear for it," she added with a nervous laugh. "I don't remember how to dance. I've only had sex with one man in my life, and he was a pretty unimaginative man. On top of all that, I'm too old for you."

He was grinning. "No, I think you're probably too young for me. But I don't care. I don't like to dance and I don't judge anybody by their underwear. And I'm damned glad you're inexperienced."

"What would I tell my kids? I've been trying to convince them that sex is only all right for married people."

He laughed. "I'll tell you a secret, Jane. They probably don't believe you. And what you tell them is that when they are thirty-seven—"

"Thirty-nine."

"—thirty-nine, they can do anything they want. *Les Misérables* or *The Fantasticks?*"

"What?"

"Which would you rather see?"

Jane put her head on his shoulder and didn't say anything for a long time. Her mother-in-law would have a fit if she went away for a weekend with Mel.

"*The Fantasticks*," she finally said very softly.

Todd came hurtling through the French doors a few minutes later to tattle on his brother. "Mom, Mike says—Oh, iiiccckkk! Kissing!"

Sort of chokes you up to think of pitching it all."

"That's Ted's room," Shelley said.

"Dead Ted?" Jane asked.

"Dead Ted! That sounds like a rock group," Edgar said, laughing uneasily.

"Ted Francisco," Shelley said. "I guess I better explain to both of you—just in case anything awkward happens."

"Are you anticipating 'something awkward'?" Jane asked.

Edgar looked distinctly unhappy at this turn in the conversation.

Shelley didn't answer directly. "This house belonged to Judge Francisco. He and his wife had a son Ted, who was in our class in high school. He was handsome, smart, athletic, everything. We were all madly in love with him. He had everything going for him." She paused for a moment before finishing. "The night of our senior prom, he committed suicide."

"Where?" Edgar asked quietly.

Shelley pointed above them. "In that room."

"Another cream puff?" Edgar asked Jane solicitously. They were back in the bright, cheerful kitchen. Hector was lashing himself against Jane's legs.

"My thighs will have to have their own zip code if I eat another," Jane said. She turned to Shelley. "How did he do it? Dead Ted, I mean."

"Carbon monoxide. Besides the stairway upstairs, there's a sort of hatch at the back of the garage. It opened next to Ted's bed. It used to be a joke with us. Ted could be out of there as fast as a fireman, flinging up the hatch, sliding down a rope almost into the front seat of his car. Anyway, that night he left the car running and the hatch open. His parents were out of town overnight and when they came back, they found him fully dressed in bed. Dead. It was horrible for them. He was literally the light of their lives. An only child, born to them when they were in their late forties, I believe. Judge Francisco had a complete breakdown. By the time he recovered, his wife had closed the house and they moved away. I didn't realize they'd left Ted's room just like it was. I guess they couldn't stand to get rid of his things and just walked away and left it."

"Do you think this is why the house was vacant for so long?" Edgar asked. "We bought it from their estate."

"My guess is that they couldn't make themselves come back to the house, but couldn't bear to sell it either," Shelley said. "So they're both dead. Not surprising. They were a much older couple than the rest of our parents. They had Ted very late in life."

"It's a shame the house was left to stand vacant so long. It's a lovely place," Jane said.

"It wasn't so lovely when we got it," Edgar said. "In fact, I wouldn't have gone along with buying it if Gordon hadn't been so confident that something could be made of it. There had been transients living here off and on and the police told us—after we bought it, of course—that a drug ring had been operating out of here. Why, some of the riffraff have even turned up since we moved in. One night, we heard scrabbling noises and came down to find a young couple in what you might call 'a delicate situation' right in the middle of the living room. Thrashing around in a pile of sawdust. That's why we're awfully fussy about keeping the doors locked at night. We're going to ask guests to be in by ten-thirty or they'll have to wake us to get in."

"There must be a lot of details to work out when

you're opening a place like this," Jane said.

"Probably a lot more that we haven't even thought of yet. But your group will be a nice trial run, Shelley. I'm sure it's going to go wonderfully well," Edgar said with determined brightness.

Jane was surprised that Shelley didn't answer, but continued to stare out the window at the rain. She was frowning. It was always a bad sign when Shelley frowned. "I hope I haven't made a big mistake," she said, more to herself than to them.

# —— 3 ——

Wednesday morning was wildly hectic. Jane's car pool schedule—as elaborate as a schedule of Mafia debts, her Uncle Jim claimed—fell to pieces. The mother who was supposed to drive Jane's high school son Mike's car pool called sounding like she was in the final stages of pneumonia and tried to get Jane to take her place.

"I'm sorry, but I've got the grade school this week and the whole junior high group has come down with something and I've got to drive my daughter, too. I'm really sorry, but you'll just have to press your husband into service," Jane said firmly. She probably would have caved in and helped if it had been humanly possible. It would have put the other driver under a terrific obligation. Being owed a car pool favor wasn't to be taken lightly.

"Oh, Jane, you know what an idiot Stan is about car pools."

"Stan runs a whole bank! He's just convinced you he's too stupid to figure out how to drive the kids so you won't ask him to help," Jane said. "It's selective idiocy. Steve used to do the same thing."

There was some more sniffling and whining at the other end. Jane sympathized. Her own late husband Steve, who had died in a car accident a year and a half earlier, had been just as discriminately parental.

20